Lost Diaries
and Other Short Stories

Also by this author

Tales From Here There and Everywhere

Human Response To Tall Buildings

Lost Diaries
and Other Short Stories

by
Don Conway

ISBN: 978-0-692-12024-8

PublishNation LLC
www.publishnation.net

For my son Russell

ACKNOWLEDGEMENTS

Critique, feedback and much love from the Royal Palm Beach Writers Group made this project possible.

Russell Conway and Kathi Conway were my "Go for it" team. Many thanks.

CONTENTS

PROLOGUE

What if you could place yourself in the Moulin Rouge cabaret in the Pigalle section of Paris at the height of the Belle Époque in 1889. Wouldn't you go there...at least in your mind's eye?

How about crossing the Delaware River with George Washington or fighting against apartheid with Nelson Mandela. Would you like to give those a try? I thought you would.

And so would I. That's why I've written these ten fictional Lost Diary stories. I have made every effort to ensure that all historical references are accurate. Any errors in this book are mine and mine alone. There are no lost diaries but by studying these ten people and their place in history I have —in my minds eye, — taken these trips back in time.

Join me. All you have to do is step inside these pages.

Don Conway, Florida 2018

THE LOST DIARY OF

TOULOUSE-LAUTREC

For many years there has been speculation that the artist Toulouse-Lautrec (**TL**) kept a personal diary. Following his death on September 9, 1901 due to the combined effects of syphilis and alcoholism, his personal effects were taken over by his mother. She was determined to promote the artistic works of her unfortunate son. No diary was found at that time however the rumor of its existence persisted.

In 2015 a descendent of Rosa La Rouge, a Parisian prostitute with whom TL had lived from 1886 to1887 came upon his diary among La Rouge's belongings. The long-lost diary of TL had been found at last.

The last entry in the diary is dated Wednesday, May 19, 1886— a momentous day in the artist's life as told in his own words. That entry is presented here.

Wednesday

May 19, 1886

Dr. Mathieu has confirmed his original diagnosis. I have the Pox*

I have no doubt that I contracted it from Rosa...not that that matters. I think she does not even know she has it. I must speak to her about this. Poor Rosa. I must also send a personal warning to Oscar.** He is living on the edge.

The Doctor has explained that there is no cure for the Pox, only treatments with Mercury. They sound as horrible as the disease itself and there are high risks for disastrous side effects and early death due to Mercury poisoning.

No! I will not undergo the indignity and torment of these Mercury treatments.

The Doctor says it will take ten to fifteen years for the disease to kill me. And it will be an ugly and unpleasant death. So be it. There is always Absinth and more Earthquakes***.

If I have ten to fifteen years to continue my work then I shall make the most of them.

Of course, I must explain all of this to Momma. She worries about me so and this news will add to her burden. It is bad enough that she has had to deal with The Old Fool**** for all these years. It is ironic that I should be the one to come down with the Pox. With all his years of womanizing and humiliating Momma it is a wonder that he, who so deserves it, did not catch this disease first. Another of life's injustices...

Had Alphonse*****, lived and not been a dwarf such as I am, he would have been able to provide Momma with some consolation.

Now I must look to my own future with some measure of practicality. Will my dear friends at the near-by brothels continue to service me? I think that if I procure a supply of the new rubber condoms they will. In their wisdom they are bound to see that this disease is only one more of the manifestations that sets them, and me, apart from the rest of Society. The world of prostitutes, dancers, dwarfs and circus performers, our world, is so afflicted with damaged human beings that the Pox will not make a significant difference to them.

And so, if I continue to be accepted in our world, I will be able to bear witness, through my work, to the fact that though we are society's outcasts, we are also human beings.

Ten or fifteen more years of paintings, drawings and lithographs may not be enough to teach this lesson to the world but I have no choice but to try to make the rest of humanity see the real us...and me.

* The Pox was a common term for Syphilis in the 1800's

** Oscar Wilde whom TL had befriended and who was later tried for homosexuality and served two years in a British prison. He died alone and destitute in Paris in 1900

*** Earthquakes were a drink invented by TL consisting of 1 part Absinth and 1part Cognac.

**** The Old Fool was TL's pejorative for his father with whom he had a contentious relationship.

***** Alphonse was TL's younger brother who died at an early age.

THE LOST DIARY OF

GEORGE WASHINGTON

American History scholars have been ecstatic over the finding of George Washington (GW) long suspected, but never found, diaries written during the Revolutionary War years. GW was a lifelong diarist. His diaries from 1768 through 1789 have been found, analyzed and reproduced for many years. All his diaries and thousands of personal papers are cataloged and transcribed by the University of Virginal Library.

Oddly, though, the only known copies of his diaries stop in June 1776 and are not resumed until 1789 when he assumed the presidency. For years, scholars have wondered why such an ardent and disciplined diarist did not maintain his diary during some of the most critical years of his life —the Revolutionary war years.

It is understandable then, why American History scholars were excited and delighted when his war years diary was accidentally found in 2015 during some restoration work at Mount Vernon. The news of the finding was widely publicized in 2015 but none of the material was released to the public until an extensive investigation and examination were completed to assure the authenticity of the diary. That work has now been completed and given the title of George Washington's Revolutionary War Diary.

In this paper, we are presenting just one entry from that diary to give the reader a glimpse into his mindset, emotions and writing style on December 25th, 1776 the eve of a crucial event i.e. the battle of Trenton, New Jersey. The actual battle took place the following day, December 26th.

We feel it is useful to place December 25th into the overall context in which Washington found himself and his army on that day.

We start on July 3rd, 1775 When Washington was given command of the Continental Army and he joined the revolutionary forces in their siege of Boston. In a word, he was shocked at the size, condition, and structure of the forces he found surrounding Boston. At this point, General Washington had to both form his forces into an army and defeat the British holding Boston under the command of General Sir William Howe.

We do not have any information about how GW went about shaping his army but we do know how he dealt with the British. In the first of many brilliant and daring actions, he managed, in a single night, to move much of his army and all of it's artillery to Dorchester heights above Boston. With the American artillery on Dorchester Heights, General Howe faced annihilation, surrender or retreat. He chose to retreat. Howe loaded his entire army onto British warships anchored in Boston harbor and set sail for Halifax, Nova Scotia, Canada.

With Boston freed from the British occupation, Washington anticipated Howe's next move would be to try to capture New York (City). In preparation for the British attack on New York Washington marched his entire army to Long Island (Brooklyn) and Manhattan Island. The battles of Long Island and New York in July-August 1776 did not go well for Washington. Seriously outnumbered by more than 25,000 British and Hessian troops, and a fleet of 400 British ships in New York Harbor, Washington was forced into a series of strategic retreats out of Long Island and up the full length of Manhattan island. It must be noted however that in effecting his army's retreat from Brooklyn, across the East River and into Manhattan, Washington managed the equivalent of the WWII evacuation of Dunkirk. GW accomplished this retreat in one night using rowed barges to carry men, horses, and artillery across the river.

Retreating as best he could, Washington finally gained the heights above the Hudson River where he had established forts on either side of it: Fort Washington on the New York side, and Fort Lee on the New Jersey side. With these two forts commanding the Hudson River narrows, the British fleet was forced to turn and sail back to New York harbor. This move gave Washington time to move his army across the Hudson into New Jersey.

The following months, August to October 1776 saw GW's army being pursued Southward through New Jersey by overwhelming British and Hessian troops. In October, he moved his army across the Delaware River into Pennsylvania. His camp was about ten miles North of Trenton, New Jersey. He stopped at this point to regroup his army and to await the arrival of General Charles Lee with 4,000 troops. By this time, winter was approaching and, in the style of European armies, General Howe ceased his active pursuit of Washington and retired to New York for the winter.

In this narrative, we are now approaching December 25, 1776. With the bulk of the British army in New York, we can now pause to consider Washington's situation.

The defeat at the battle of Long Island and the harried retreat through New York and New Jersey left Washington's army in dire straits. On the first of December, the enlistment's of most of his soldiers was up and more that three thousand left the army to return to their homes. Those that remained, about 2,400, were sickly, under supplied and demoralized.

Enter now the figure of General Charles Lee Washington most experienced General. When Washington started his retreat through New Jersey he left General Lee at Fort Lee on the New Jersey Heights above the Hudson river. (Fort Lee had been named in honor of General Lee.) The plan was that General Lee would form a rear guard to protect Washington retreating army. Once GW had established his winter camp General Lee was to join him with 4,000 badly needed troops.

There was a problem. General Lee had served in the British, Polish and Portuguese armies in a number of European wars. His military experience was far greater than Washington's. When the Continental Congress started debating the leadership of the Continental Army General Lee expected to be appointed its Commanding General. Washington's appointment, for valid political reasons, left Lee a bitter and reluctant member of Washington's army. He seemed to express this by dawdling and delaying his New Jersey retreat behind Washington's army. In letters from Washington to Lee, we know that Lee was aware of the poor condition of Washington's troops and the necessity of Lee's 4,000 men to join up with the main body of the army. Due to his lax behavior and poor judgment, General Lee was captured by a small British patrol on December 10, 1776, He was out of the war until he was released in a prisoner exchange in 1781

The next person we must consider in understanding GW's mindset on December 25th is Colonel Joseph Reed. Reed was a Pennsylvania-born lawyer and politician who eventually became the Governor of Pennsylvania. During the Revolutionary war, he served as the Adjutant-General (AG) of the army with the rank of Colonel. The AG is the

Chief Administrative Officer of the Army who traditionally serves as the key assistant and principal adviser to the Commander in Chief. There is reason to believe that a strong bond of friendship existed between the GW and Reed. It may not be an exaggeration to say that Joseph Reed provided GW with some form of comradeship if not emotional support during this trying period.

On the afternoon of December 24th, quite by accident, Washington came into some delayed letters between General Lee and Colonel Reed. The crux of these letters was to share expressions of concern about Washington's competence as the leader of the army.

The following entry from Washington's diary, written on the afternoon of December 25th tells us of his reaction to these revelations from two of his most important military subordinates.

Bucks County, Pa., 25 December 1776

The General Orders for the Army have been issued & we are as prepared as we can be for tomorrow's strike against Trenton. If we succeed in causing much misery to the Hessian garrison we will immediately turn our efforts to Princeton village.

I place some store on these encounters to overcome the damage to the army's image engendered by our unfortunate issues in New

York & the retreat through New Jersey.

Considering the size, state and moral of our troops a victory in the above conflicts may do much to alter these factors.

Letters between General Lee and Colonel Reed, which have recently come to hand, reveal their mutual loss of loyalty and faith in my abilities as Cmndr. in Chief of the army. There may be some within the Continental Congress who share their beliefs.

I will not undertake to determine what will be

the result of these ill -judged thoughts, but this I

think may be said—my devotion to our sac red

cause allows me to press forward without due

concern for these external matters.

And now the hour has come for us to cross the

Delaware and make our strike on Trenton village.

George Washington's brilliant victories at Trenton and Princeton turned the thoughts of Americans from near despair to the possibility of a final victory over the British.

THE LOST DIARY OF

MARIE ANTOINETTE

Marie Antoinette, the Queen of France and wife of Louis XVI, was guillotined on October 16th, 1793. Her execution followed fourteen months in a variety of prisons in the Paris area. Her final cell was in the dungeon of La Conciergerie where she was transferred for her trial by the Revolutionary Tribunal. Her prayer book, pen, ink, and paper were available to her during her incarceration. Following her execution, her prayer book was turned over to the Revolutionary Tribunal and eventually made its way to the Louvre museum where it resides today. It was widely speculated that the Queen kept a secret diary during her months in prison but no trace of it could be found until 2015 when it was discovered in a trunk in the attic of an obscure apartment building in Paris.

The diary covers the period from the fall of the monarchy, in August 1792, until the day of her execution in 1793. The final, poignant, entry written in the early morning hours while she waited for her executioner, is presented here.

4:30 am, October 16, 1793

It is only a matter of hours now.

How do I tell the world of a life such as mine of the rise from Austrian, Hapsburg princess to Queen of France to a prisoner in a cold, dark, rat-infested dungeon? How do I tell the world of the meaning of such a life? My marriage to Louis XVI at the age of fourteen cast me into a fantasy world. Yes, I indulged myself in all the pleasures his fortune and my position allowed. And many that were not allowed but which I took anyway. My beautiful Hans, * the sensuous Duchesse de Polignac**, the Petit Trianon, exaggerated hairstyles and extravagant dresses. Yes, I took advantage of all of them but they had no meaning for me. Meaning came into my life after the birth of my children. It was only then that I began to understand the responsibilities of a Queen. I did, I really did, try to concern myself with the well-being of my subjects. But I am Austrian, and they are French. There was so much about them that I could not grasp and by this stage in my life my reputation was too far soiled to be accepted by the French. And so I go to my death finally understanding that a true Queen must forsake her own life and wishes and devoted herself to the welfare of her country, even this adopted one, and its people. And so it seems the meaning of my life must be to serve as *an example for all persons of power. You are nothing. Humanity is everything.*

They are coming for me now. Auf Wiedersehen zum Leben ***

* Hans Axel von Fersen was a Swedish soldier and Marie Antoinette lover for many years starting in 1774 while she was Queen of France.

** The Duchesse de Polignac was Marie Antoinette lesbian lover for many years.

*** Goodbye to life.

THE LOST DIARY OF

JESUS CHRIST

Jesus Christ was crucified on Friday, April 3, 33 AD*. He kept a diary which Mary Magdalene his, perhaps, wife/girlfriend, held for him for safekeeping. When she faded out of history, shortly after the crucifixion, the diary was lost with her. It was discovered in Syria in 2000 to the great joy of biblical scholars. Because of its historical and religious significance, the diary was kept secret until 2017 when it was finally confirmed to be the actual diary of Jesus Christ. David Ben Gurion University in Israel translated the original from the Aramaic language in 2016. The Israeli government wanted this text to be widely disseminated to, and accepted by, the general population. For this reason, the translation was done and presented in the popular vernacular of 2017. While this may seem strange for a religious text "acceptance" was given precedence over "accuracy".

Jesus was thirty-three years old when he was crucified. The diary covers his life from his "walk on water", and assembly of the Apostles, until five days before his crucifixion. His last entry, on March 29, 33 AD, is presented here.

March 29, 33 AD

So far, the enterprise is going well. The old religious men, the keepers of the Temple, are the only ones who are giving us any problems. The Zionists' resistance to the Romans is causing the administration to tighten security and, despite our efforts not to be associated with that rebellion; the Temple guys are trying to convince Pontius Pilot that we are part of their uprising. This could be a problem in the next couple of days.

In the meantime, we are doing well. I find that after I do my sermon thing and leave the collections to Big James, the hot head, and a mean looking guy, plus John and my cousin Little Jimmy, they really bringing in the shekels.

As a matter of fact, since the purse is full, I've decided to treat the whole crew to a supper. I've rented the upper room of a building in Jerusalem (it's cheaper than the lower floor) for the event. Nothing elaborate. Probably just some bread, wine and a bit of cheese. Since Matthew is our money guy, I am leaving the arrangements. to him. Pete agrees this is a good idea but, as usual, doubting Thomas has his reservations. Still, I am going ahead with it.

Mariam is giving me a hard time about this. I've explained to her that this is a guy thing, but she insists on coming. Our relationship is pretty hot right now, and I don't want to give her up. So, I suppose I'll have to let her come. Women! Who can reason with them? It's certainly beyond my power.

*Authors note: The reader may be interested to know that his date of birth has been authoritatively placed as Saturday, April 17, 6 BC.

THE LOST DIARY OF

FRIDA KAHLO

Frida Kahlo, artist, wife of Diego Rivera, and symbol of Mexican womanhood, was born July 6, 1907 and died July 13, 1954 in the same house in Coyoacán, Mexico. Her house is now the Museo de Frida Kahlo. For almost thirty of her forty-seven years, she lived in pain and suffering. Her physical pain was due to a horrific accident when she was eighteen years old. She was tormented by several back surgeries, a deformed right leg, several abortions, and miscarriages. Her inner, psychological suffering was the result of her tempestuous, off-again, on-again marriage and total devotion to Diego Rivera.

They were married in 1929, divorced in 1938, and remarried in 1940. Frida tolerated Diego's many infidelities while he was consumed with jealousy over her many, many affairs which included several lesbian lovers. Their marriage suffered from sharp differences in their psychological make-ups, financial difficulties, partly due to Frida's lifelong medical expenses and, in the beginning, Frida's having to live under the shadow of Mexico's greatest muralist. By the 1940's, their positions began to be reversed. The great Mexican Muralist Period of 1920-1950 was fading, while Frida's artistic career was just reaching its zenith.

For all their adult lives, Freda and Diego were devoted and active Communists, though there were a few years when they were expelled from the party, because of their aid to Leon Trotsky. Eventually, however, both were reinstated as party members. While most of Diego's murals celebrated Communist themes, Frida's paintings were mainly self-portraits that reflected her own inner feelings and inner turmoil. From her early adulthood, Frida cultivated a public image of a Tehuana or Mexican peasant woman — the classic heroic sufferer. For most of her adult life, she wore the long colorful skirts, blouses, and rebosos of lower class Mexican women. This is the image of Frida that is most commonly associated with her to this day.

Starting in the 1940's, when her career gained momentum, Frida– always aware of her pending death– began to realize that she would be leaving a legacy of paintings, letters, colorful costumes, and her "public" diary etc. to the Mexican people. Secretly, however, she kept a "private" diary in which she recorded the intimate details of her life, her love for Diego, and her lifelong struggle against pain. As far as is known, the only person who was aware of her secret diary was her longtime nurse, friend, and companion Judith Ferreto. It was Ferreto who found Frida's body on July 13, 1954. Though her death certificate stated the cause of death as coronary thrombosis, Ferreto, who kept count of Frida's medications, implied that she had committed suicide with an overdose of pain medications.

It is apparent that upon Frida's death, Ferreto kept the secret diary. When Ferreto died in 1972, the secret diary was found among her possessions. The poignant entry from that diary, which is presented here, is dated August 22, 1953, the evening before Frida was to have her right leg amputated.

Aug. 22, 1953

About 11 pm

Tomorrow Dr. Velasco y Polo is going to cut off

my right leg.

For more than 25 years death has been stalking

me. Step by step and inch by inch he has Tortured

me with pain. Tomorrow will be a big victory for

death as he begins to dismember my body piece by piece. I wonder how long it will take him to complete the job? Perhaps it is time for me to cheat death and take the easy way out.* Diego says he cannot live without me in his life. In many ways, he is terribly fragile. I do not think I can inflict my death on him. I know he will suffer and I cannot bear to cause him pain. No! I must continue to put up with my own pain in order to save him. When he came to visit me this evening** it twisted my heart to see his anguish over my condition.

So I will continue to live and paint. That is just as well since I have not completed my message to the world about the injustices of Capitalism and the plight of the working man. The Party seems to be grateful and is using some of my paintings, and my reputation, to its advantage.

The loss of my leg only causes me to reaffirm the passions that govern my Life — painting,

Diego, the Party, Mexico and my own life. So

much yet to do and say about each of these.

Viva la Vida!

* She did not commit suicide at this time.

** Though they were married Frida and Diego were living in separate houses.

THE LOST DIARY OF

NELSON MANDELA

At the beginning of 1961, the South African Government
issued a warrant for Nelson Mandela's arrest.

Now a fugitive from justice, he was forced to go
underground to continue his activities for the African
National Congress (ANC). Perhaps this was just as well
since he was undergoing a profound change in his
thinking about the policies and activities of the ANC. He
was about to attempt to persuade the organization to
abandon its fifty-year policy of non-violence, modeled
after Gandhi's success in India, to one of militant
resistance against the government. This is well
documented in his autobiography *Long Walk to
Freedom.*

Mandela was a meticulous lawyer, accustomed to keeping records of all his activities on behalf of the ANC. He even kept a diary of his day-to-day professional activities. What was not known was that he also kept a personal diary, in which he recorded and revealed many of his inner thoughts and feelings.

His personal diary only came to light after the death of his son Makgatho in 2005. The diary was found by his grandchildren amongst Makgatho's personal belongings.

The last entry in his personal diary is dated June 20, 1961, and records his rational and decision for convincing the ANC to abandon its policy of non-violence.

Some historical background will help the reader understand this entry.

When the ANC was founded in 1912, its leaders believed in two things: the fairness of the British government and the non-violence strategies of Mahatma Gandhi. For the next fifty years, the ANC used letters, personal appeals, manifestoes, strikes and stay-at-home campaigns to try to gain rights and freedoms for Africans.

To no avail. In fact, the SA Government increased the laws and regulations governing Africans, to strengthen its policy of Apartheid.

On March 21, 1960, Government police were attempting to remove 150 families from a township called Sharpsville. Africans protested, nonviolently, but the police deliberately opened fire on the civilians. Sixty-nine men, women and children were killed and more that 200 were injured. The incident became known as the Sharpsville Massacre. Mandela has stated in his autobiography that this was the beginning of his conviction that the nonviolence strategy had lost its usefulness.

Similar incidents and the increasing violence of the police and military under the presidency of Hendrik Verwoerd into 1961 convinced Mandela that violence was the only alternative left for the ANC.

In June 1961, Mandela met with the National Executive Committee of the ANC at a secret meeting in Durban. In a marathon meeting and debate, he eventually got permission to form a militant organ, called The Spear of the Nation, to undertake strikes against the government. The following entry in his personal diary, dated June 20, 1961, reveals some of Mandela's thoughts and fears about the new policy.

June 20, 1961

Yesterday I argued, begged and pleaded with the Executive Committee for a change in direction for the ANC. I am acutely aware of how momentous a decision this is for us...but the government has left us no alternative. I now have permission to form an underground army as an arm of the ANC. At the outset we will strike at the instruments and institutions of the government such as telephone services, railroads, and police stations. We will not target people.

All of this is new to me. I am not a soldier, and I have never fired a gun at anyone. I will have to find and recruit peoples with experience in explosives, guerrilla warfare, and logistics. How does one create, arm, and maintain a secret army? Much to learn and to do.

It is essential that we inform the public of this new direction. The brutality and increasing frequency of the government's attacks on townships and homelands have left the public demoralized and feeling helpless. They must know that they/we will no longer sit idly by and suffer this oppression but will hit back.

I have drafted a letter* which I will release to the newspapers on the 26th. In it, I explain our new direction and entreat the public, Africans, Whites, Indians and

Coloreds to join us in this resistance movement.

*The letter was sent to all the leading newspapers in South Africa on June 26, 1961. Copy follows.

I am informed that a warrant has been issued for my arrest and that the police are looking for me. The National Action Council has given full and serious consideration to this question...and they have advised me not to surrender myself. I have accepted this advice and will not give myself up to a Government I do not recognize. Any serious politician will realize that under present day conditions in the country, to seek for cheap martyrdom by handing myself to the police is naïve and criminal....

I have chosen this course which is more difficult, and which entails more risk and hardship than sitting in gaol. I have had to separate myself from my dear wife and children, from my mother and sisters to live as an outlaw in my own land. I have had to close my business, to abandon my profession, and live in poverty, as many of my people are doing...I shall fight the Government side by side with you, inch by inch, and mile by mile, until victory is won.

What are you going to do? Will you come along with us, or are you going to co-operate with the Government in its efforts to suppress the claims and aspirations of your own people? Are you going to remain silent and neutral in a matter of life and death to my people, to our people? For my part I have made my choice. I will not leave South Africa, nor will I surrender. Only through hardship, sacrifice and militant action can freedom be won. The struggle is my life. I will continue fighting for freedom until the end of my days.

Authors Note: Nelson Mandela was arrested, tried and, on June 13, 1964, sentenced to life in prison. He was released twenty-seven years later on February 11, 1990.

THE LOST DIARY OF

ELIZABETH CADY STANTON

From Wikipedia:

Elizabeth Cady Stanton (November 12, 1815 - October 26, 1902) was an American suffragist, social activist, abolitionist, and leading figure of the early women's rights movement. Her Declaration of Sentiments, presented at the Seneca Falls Convention held in 1848 in Seneca Falls, New York, is often credited with initiating the first organized women's rights and women's suffrage movements in the United States. Stanton was president of the National Woman Suffrage Association from 1892 until 1900.

Susan B. Anthony is often credited with founding the woman's rights movement in the United States. However she and Elizabeth Stanton were lifelong friends and co-workers in both the slavery abolitionist movement and woman's rights movements. Following the end of the Civil war in 1865, they focused their attentions on woman's rights. It may be said that Elizabeth Stanton provided the philosophical and legal direction to the movement while Susan Anthony was its visible face. Susan Anthony was often quoted as saying, "Elizabeth developed the thunderbolts which I fired."

Elizabeth Stanton was married and had a husband and several children to look after. Susan was unmarried and free to travel and represent the cause at meetings around the country, before the U.S. Congress and, when necessary, going to jail for her activities.. This difference in their circumstances probably accounts for the public's perception of Anthony as the principal representative of the Suffragette movement.

Stanton's father was a lawyer and Justice of the New York Supreme Court. It has been said that he sometimes wished he had had a son. Perhaps it was this wish that caused him to coach young Elizabeth in the rudiments of the law and allowed her to mingle with the other lawyers and law clerks in his office.

By the age of thirty-three, in 1848, she was a seasoned advocate for both the abolition of slavery and the nascent woman's rights movement. In that year she joined a group of Quaker women in Seneca Falls, New York in organizing "a convention to discuss the social, civil, and religious condition and rights of woman." It was held in Seneca Falls on July 19 and 20, 1848, two years before Elizabeth met Susan B. Anthony.

The Seneca Falls Convention is generally identified as the start of the woman's rights movement in the United States.

As a principle speaker, Elizabeth Stanton delivered a, now famous speech, and a document, entitled A Declaration of Rights and Sentiments which was modeled after the U.S. Declaration of Independence. The convention adopted her Declaration and one hundred participants signed it. Following the convention, Fredrick Douglas promoted the Declaration as a, "grand movement for attaining the civil, social, political, and religious rights of women."

Perhaps because of her awareness of the inflammatory nature of the Declaration Stanton kept a secret diary in which she contemplated the importance of the document, its possible social consequences and the potential effect it might have on her life and family situation. The diary was lost and not seen again until after her death in 1902. The entry presented here is dated July 16, 1848, three days before her presentation at the Seneca Falls Convention.

Sunday   July 16, 1848

Most of the preparations for the convention

are completed. Only the construction of the

speakers platform and its patriotic bunting

remain to be finished. The Quaker-ladies are even now preparing the refreshments we will serve following the speeches.

For the tenth time I have reread my own presentation. I am satisfied that I have copied the structure of the Declaration of Independence. I believe that by doing so I have added strength and justification to the grievances I am claiming and the resolutions that I will be proposing. But I keep wondering if it is too aggressive? Have I unjustly criticized all men? Certainly, I know there are good men in this world. And yet, even the best of men, or should I say the most of men, have fallen into the mind-set of oppressing women. I blame the social pressure of our times as much as any overtly malicious interest in doing harm to women...still, they continue to see us as less than full citizens...almost as slaves. This cannot continue!

My sincerest hope is that my Declaration of Rights and Sentiments will be taken seriously and given full consideration. If we can persuade the New York state legislature to accept and act upon some of the resolutions I am presenting, which should result in changes in the voting, divorce and property rights of women in this state, then perhaps it will serve as a model and legal precedent for other states to follow. This will be a long and arduous fight. It is not likely that I will live to see the miracle of universal suffrage for women in the United States.

More immediately, I am concerned for the consequences that releasing the Declaration may hold for my family and me. Will local women, even some of our friends and family, consider my husband, my children and me as outcast of society? Are there some hidden financial punishments that local banks and businesses can inflict upon us?

Yes, I worry about these things...but the cause of woman's rights is too great...I must go on.

THE LOST DIARY OF

LINDA LOVELACE

Linda Susan Boreman, aka Linda Lovelace, left the porn industry in 1980 after the birth of her second child. That was the year her biography, Ordeal, was published. In that same year, she joined and became active in, the anti-pornography movement. Ordeal was the third of four biographies written, or co-written by her. The others were: Inside Linda Lovelace (1974), The Intimate Diary of Linda Lovelace (1974) and Out of Bondage (1986). Despite these publications, and because of her Catholic school upbringing, there were intimate details of her life that she only revealed to herself in a secret diary. She began keeping her secret diary shortly after she gave birth to an illegitimate child when she was about twenty years old. It covers her first automobile accident in 1969, her marriage to Chuck Traynor, who coerced her into prostitution and pornography, the filming of Deep Throat in 1972, and the stardom that followed. She also chronicled the downward spiral of her acting career through the late 1970's and early 80's and her marriage to a Long Island cable installer in 1974.

Her life on Long Island seemed to provide her with a sense of normalcy and comfort with the birth of her two children in 1977 and 1980. Her first serious health issue came up in those same years when she was required to have a liver transplant as a result of her 1969 automobile accident. In subsequent years she was to undergo a double mastectomy, and towards the end of her life, she was receiving dialysis treatments due to kidney problems. She was driving to her dialysis treatment on April 2, 2002, the day of her fatal automobile accident. The story of Linda's life is a roller coaster morality tale of marital abuse, porn-queen stardom, drug problems, and born-again Christendom. Her anti-pornography evangelism took her to the halls of Congress where she testified at government hearings on pornography. She maintained an active speaking schedule at college campuses and before feminist groups.

Her secret diary was not discovered until after her death. Linda's last entry is dated Sunday, March 26, 2002, eight days before her fatal accident and twenty-eight days before she was taken off life support and died. Linda Borman is buried in Parker Cemetery in Parker, Colorado.

March 26, 2002

Dear Diary,

Hello again, it's me, Linda. Yes, I know, it has been awhile since my last entry. This time I'll blame my darned dialysis treatments. Honestly, diary, they are a drag. Five days a week I must lay for hours on that lumpy bed, in a cold, clammy room and have my system flushed. My doctor says these treatments are keeping me alive, so there is nothing to do but grin and bear it. On a brighter note, I can tell you that this past Christmas was a *wonderful time for the whole family. My grandchildren—the lights of my life—were the center of it all. Larry* even came by with presents for the grand kids. I must give him credit: he has been a good friend ever since our divorce and that was six years ago.1*

Here's a bit of news for you. I just heard that Herb** has finally found Jesus! Can you imagine that? I hope his new-found religion will give him the restitution and comfort that God has given me. I bear him no grudges and wish him well.

I recently did a photo shoot for Leg Show magazine. Leg show is a kind of soft-porn magazine. All I did were a couple of lingerie pictures for them. I agreed to let them use my name on the cover which they think will help their sales. I must admit it was nice to be back in a photo studio again. The magazine people were nice to me, even if they didn't pay much. The photography staff was courteous and polite. It was all very professional and a much-needed boost for my 53-year-old ego.

The Women Against Pornography group has been in touch with me again. They want me to come back and be part of their speaker's bureau. I know they get thousands of dollars in donations due to my participation but all I get is a measly five hundred dollars or so for my ninety-minute presentation. And I get nothing for travel, hotel or food expenses. Like so many others in my life, I resent their "using me." So, I have turned them down. Never again!

I continue to make presentations to women's groups and on college campuses. When I speak to a group of women, I can feel the empathy in the room and see it in their eyes, and I feel like my message is getting through to them. The college kids are another matter. Some of the young women seem to get it. Others appear to be indifferent to the things I have had to bear...as if it were my fault or something I chose to do on my own. Even when I explain to them that Chuck*** practically held a gun to my head all during the shooting of DT. They seem to be a hard lot of women. I wonder what their lives will *be like. The male college students are the worst. I know they come to my presentation almost hoping I will do "it" for them. Some just want the notoriety of shaking my hand so they can brag in the dorms that they touched Linda Lovelace.*

Please God, deliver me from my past.

*Larry Marchiano. Linda's second husband (1974-1996) and friend following their divorce. He was at her bedside when she died.

**Herbert Streicher aka Harry Reems. Linda's co-star in Deep Throat

***Chuck Traynor. Linda's first husband and pimp (1971-1974)

THE LOST DIARY OF

ROBERT E. LEE

In June 1862 General Robert E. Lee was appointed the commander of the Northern Army of the Confederate States. He renamed his new army the Army of Northern Virginia. It was considered by most to be the principal army of the Confederacy. Up until that appointment, his military career received mixed reviews. As a West Point graduate and a thirty-two-year veteran of the United States Army, Lee's principal activities were as an army engineer. As a young brevet major he had distinguished himself in the Mexican-American war of 1846-48 where, by the way, he met and worked alongside Ulysses S. Grant. Following that war, Lee held a variety of positions in the U.S. Army including Superintendent of the U.S. Military Academy at West Point. As a slave owner and manager of his father-in-law's plantation, he was involved in a notorious event known as the Norris Case in which Lee was accused of whipping a female slave with his own hand. The evidence against him was non-conclusive, but the stigma of the incident followed him for the rest of his life.

Before the 1862 appointment, he had been defeated in several early Civil War battles. His reputation was that of a brilliant tactician and field commander but a weak strategic officer. All of that seemed to fall away from General Lee when he took command of the Army of Northern Virginia, At a variety of famous battles such as the Seven Days Battle, Antietam Creek, Spotsylvania, and the Wilderness Lee scored victories against larger and better equipped Union Forces. His most disastrous defeat was at the Battle of Gettysburg in 1863. Gettysburg was the beginning of the end of the Confederacy. His loss there forced Lee to retreat into Virginia and to marshal his forces around Richmond, the capital of the Confederacy, and St. Petersburgh. He was able to defend these strong points until April 1865 when he was forced to abandon them and start his Westward retreat to Appomattox where U. S. Grant's army surrounded him and forced Lee's surrender.

Not known as an ardent diarist few records exist of anything approaching a personal diary of Robert E. Lee's. I was not until after his death that, among some of his Civil War Personal items, his long-lost diary was found. The entry present here is dated April 5, 1865, five days before his surrender to General Grant at the Appomattox Courthouse.

Wednesday, April 5, 1865

Beans and bullets, beans and bullets...am I to be defeated by the lack of beans and bullets? No, it is more likely that Phil Sheridan will be the cause of our demise. Damn the man anyway!

It has been four days since we abandoned Richmond. Four days of forced marches by half starved and ill-equipped troops, low on ammunition and even lower on moral. My rate of desertions is beyond measure. These four days of running battles against the Unionists have tested my army beyond all endurance. I must breakthrough to the South and join-up with Gen. Johnston. Food and supplies await me at the railhead at Appomattox, of this, I am assured by my forward scouts. We must take the railroad there else I grieve for the future of my army and the Confederacy.

Dear Lord help us.

THE LOST DIARY OF

ULYSSES S. GRANT

Ulysses S. Grant was known as a hard drinking, hard fighting General of the Union Army during the Civil War. His reputation as a hard drinker, though not an alcoholic, was earned early in his military career during a period of long separation from his wife and family. His drinking habits modified significantly as he matured and were not a factor during his most critical years and battles of the Civil War. Yet the reputation stayed with him Following his graduation from West Point in 1843 he served with honor during the Mexican American War of 1846-48. He distinguished himself at the battles of Monterey, Molina Del Rey, and Chapultepec and emerged from that war as a seasoned Captain in the U.S. Army. For the first time, he considered a permanent career in the military. However, the financial strains of his growing family led him to retire from the Army in 1854 to try his hand at civilian life. The several business ventures that he entered into were not successful and at one point he ended up selling firewood on street corners in St. Louis, Missouri.

With the start of the Civil War in 1861, Grant reenlisted in the Army with his former rank. Initially assigned as a quartermaster he yearned for a combat assignment. Despite his reputation as a superb equestrian and trainer of horses, it was not until 1861 that he finally got his wish. What followed were a series of critical battles in which Grant proved himself a skillful and aggressive field commander. The list of battles in which he participated is impressive: Shiloh (1862), Vicksburg (1863), Missionary Ridge (1863), The Wilderness (1864) and Cold Harbor (1864).

One notorious incident involving Grant occurred in 1862. It became known as General Order No 11. Grant had been given command of a military district which consisted of the states of Tennessee, Mississippi, and Kentucky. He became aware of a black market involving the sale of southern cotton which he believed was helping to finance the South's rebellion. He also came to believe that this trade was being run "mostly by Jews and other unprincipled traders". On December 17, 1862, he issued his General Order No. 11, which ordered the expulsion of all Jews in the three States under his jurisdiction. President Lincoln was inundated with protests from Jewish Community leaders, members of Congress and the press. Lincoln revoked the order on January 4, 1863. During his presidential campaign of 1868, Grant stated that he had issued the order as a way to control certain Jews who had caused the problem in the first place.

July 1863 saw dual victories for the Union armies at Vicksburg Under U.S. Grant's leadership, and at Gettysburg under General George Meade. While casualties were high for both the Union and the Confederacy; General Lee's defeat was the greater in that he was never able to fully replace the troops he lost at those two battles.

The battle of Cold Harbor in July 1864, lasted for thirteen days and resulted in 52,788 Union casualties as opposed to 32,907 on the Confederate side. The country and the Northern press castigated Grant for these horrendous losses and for a while referred to him as "the Butcher" In later years, as President of the United States, Grant admitted that Cold Harbor was one of the two battles he regretted most. The other was Vicksburg.

Lee's retreat from Pennsylvania into Virginia to protect Richmond, the Capital of the Confederacy. set the stage for the siege of Richmond-Petersburgh and his eventual Western retreat to Appomattox and surrender.

Mississippi State University is the repository of millions of U.S. Grant's papers covering all relevant periods of his life and Presidency. While there are a number of memoir documents nothing like a personal diary had ever been found until 2015 when a secret, "lost diary" was discovered amongst some of his Civil War belongings.

The entry shown below is dated April 6, 1865, three days before General Lee's surrender at Appomattox Courthouse.

Apr. 6, 1865

Thursday

Thank you, God, for sending me Phil Sheridan. He has been absolutely clairvoyant about General Lee's movements over these last five days. When the old Gray fox abandoned Petersburgh Sheridan rightly predicted that he would attempt to move his army South to join Johnston in North Carolina. Sheridan and his cavalry stopped him cold at Five Forks and forced the Rebs to head West. And so it has been over these last five days. Every time Lee thought he had found a way through my lines Sheridan blocked his path and drove him further West. Now I think we have the Rebs in a pincer movement between Mead at his rear and Sheridan at his front. My concern over the next two days is to get Gibbon's infantry to Appomattox in time to reinforce Sheridan. If we succeed Lee must sue for surrender and bring an end to this nightmare war.

I have begun to formulate my terms for Lee's surrender. In general, it is not my intention to punish or humiliate the Confederates. After all, following the surrender, they will be American citizens again. They must be allowed to return to their homes with dignity and some resources to begin rebuilding the South. I am inclined to allow them to keep their horses and side arms and to provide them with rations for their journey home. I have decided to Grant General Lee and his officers an amnesty following their oath not to take up arms against the Union again.

With God's blessings, we will begin to rebuild this country again.

THE BATTLE OF APPOMATTOX

Most readers are aware of Robert E. Lee's surrender to Ulysses Grant at Appomattox Courthouse which brought the Civil War to an end. What is not widely known is the dramatic story of the Battle(s) of Appomattox that led to the surrender.

The saga starts in June of 1864 when Grant laid siege to Richmond, Virginia the capitol of the Confederacy and the near-by city of Petersburg. What followed were nine months of trench warfare and almost daily bombardments of Petersburg where Lee and most of his army were dug in. Grant's strategy was to cut off the Richmond-Petersburg and the Petersburg-Weldon railroads and thereby deprive Lee of his two lines of supplies and ammunition. Grant hoped to eventually starve-out the Confederate army and force its surrender.

By the end of March 1865 Lee knew he could no longer hold out against Grants Union Army. In a desperate situation Lee decided to attempt a break through Union blockade and join up with General Johnston's Army of Tennessee in North Carolina. Lee reasoned that if he could get his army, and himself, onto the Petersburg-Weldon railroad they could make their escape. He hadn't reckoned on General Philip Sherman.

Philip Sheridan was Grants principal general and the head of the Union Calvary. From the day Lee broke out of Petersburg Sheridan seemed to be able to anticipate his every move. For the next seven days the Union and Confederate armies engaged in an East to West running battle from

Petersburg to Appomattox. It started on April 2nd, when Lee's advanced party tried to head South out of Petersburg. Sheridan's cavalry stopped its advance at Fort Gregg and a place called Five Forks. The Confederates were forced to do an about face and go back North to join Lee's main army on the North side of the Appomattox river.

With all nearby roads leading south blocked by Sheridan, Lee's only option was to head West in a desperate attempt to reach the Richmond-Danville railroad at Burkesville where supplies of food and ammunition were waiting for his harried troops. Sheridan and his swift riding cavalry arrived at Jetersville just hours ahead of Lee's army and, again, blocked Lee from going South and getting to his supply trains.

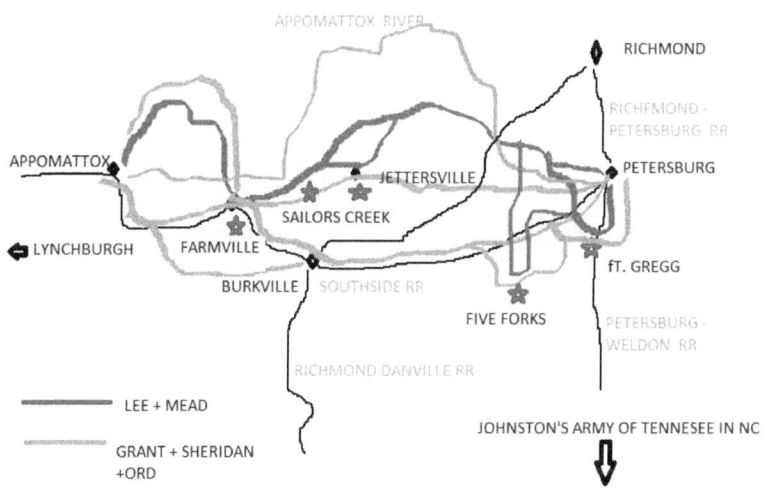

By this time, April 5th, Lee's Army of Northern Virginia was beginning to deteriorate from the grueling forced marches, lack of food and discouraged by the constant harassment of the Union troops. Once again Lee was required to head West. This time it was toward the town of Farmville and its railroad. Anticipating this move Sheridan took a parallel course and conducted several running skirmishes with Lee's ragged, but courageous, troops. There were notable battles at Sailors Creek and a place called High Bridge. And again, Sheridan was able to arrive at Farmville before the Confederates. Lee fought desperately to break through the Union Army lines to no avail. After the battle at Farmville Lee pushed Westward again this time heading for the railroad junction at Appomattox Station where, he was assured food and supplies awaited him.

It was now April 6th and General Grant saw a magnificent opportunity to spring a trap on the Southerners. With Lee's army heading West, Grant allowed it to proceed towards Appomattox. Once Lee's army had moved West and cleared the area around Farmville, Grant dispatched General Mead to take the road behind the Confederates and, through a series of attacks on the rear of Lee's army, drive it towards Appomattox. At the same time Grant sent Sheridan and his cavalry on a course parallel to Lee's but at a much faster pace. The trap was set. Mead would push the Confederates from behind and Sheridan, racing ahead would take the heights above APPOMATTOX Station and wait for Lee's army to arrive. In the meantime, Grants infantry under General Gibbon would make a forced march to Appomattox to reinforce Sheridan's cavalry.

When Lee arrived at Appomattox he sent troops up the ridge to breakthrough Sheridan's thin cavalry line. The Southerners succeeded in doing this but when they got to the top of the ridge what they saw was General Gibbon on the other side in line of battle formation. The Southerners did an about face and rode back to Lee's headquarters. With Mead behind him, and Sheridan and

Gibbon in front, of him Lee had no choice but to surrender.

The surrender took place at Appomattox Courthouse on April 9, 1865

The formal ceremony of Surrender took place on April 12th. Union Brigadier General Joshua Chamberlain was the Union officer selected to lead the ceremony. Reflecting on what he saw that day Gen. Chamberlain later wrote the following tribute:

The momentous meaning of this occasion impressed me deeply. I resolved to mark it by some token of recognition, which could be no other than a salute of arms. Well aware of the responsibility assumed, and of the criticism that would follow, as the sequel proved, nothing of that kind could move me in the least. The act could be defended, if needful, by the suggestion that such a salute was not to the cause for which the flag of the Confederacy stood, but to its going down before the flag of the Union. My main reason, however, was one for which I sought no authority nor asked forgiveness. Before us in proud humiliation stood the embodiment of manhood: men whom neither toils and sufferings, nor the fact of death, nor disaster, nor hopelessness could bend from their resolve; standing before us now, thin, worn, and famished, but erect, and with eyes looking level into ours, waking memories that bound us together as no other bond—was not such manhood to be welcomed back into a Union so tested and assured? Instructions had been given: and when the head of each division column comes opposite our group, our bugle sounds the signal and instantly our whole line from right to left, regiment by regiment in succession, gives the soldiers salutation, from "order arms" to the old "carry"—the marching salute. Gordon at the head of the column, riding with heavy spirit and down cast face, catches the sound of shifting arms, looks up, and, taking the meaning, wheels superbly, making with himself and his horse one uplifted figure with profound salutation as he drops the point of his sword to the boot toe; then facing to his own command gives word for his successive brigades to pass us with the same position of the manual, honor answering honor. On our part not a sound of trumpet more, nor roll of drum; not a cheer, nor word nor whisper of vain—glorying, nor motion of man standing again at the order, but an awed stillness rather, and breath-holding, as if it we're the passing of the dead.

Joshua L .Chamberlain, Passing of the Armies. Pp260-261

That day 27,805 Confederate soldiers passed by and stacked their arms.

CLIP-CLOP

Clip-Clop. Clip-Clop.

This is going to be tough, sergeant CB thought to herself. *Two tours in Afghanistan had been hard, but this might be harder. I guess I knew that when I volunteered for this duty. Has it only been nine weeks since I started training? So much to learn . . . caring for the horses, polishing the bridles and saddles, how to sit at attention in the saddle, the protocols for each type of funeral.*

Clip-Clop. Clip-Clop.

Well, I'm here now, officially a member of the Caisson Platoon of the Old Guard, 3rd United States Infantry. Arlington is so beautiful on a fall day like this. The sun is warm, and the trees have turned colors. And quiet. The horse's hoof beats are almost the only sound.

Clip-Clop. Clip-Clop

I'm really grateful to the Sergeant Major for stopping by the stables this morning. He knows this is my first funeral. "Not to worry CB," he said. "Just remember you're a Sergeant in the Old Guard. You know how important this ceremony is to the family. It means they can finally bring closure to this difficult time. Your job is to maintain the dignity of the funeral. That's how we show the family that we are sharing their loss." That was really helpful.

Clip-Clop. Clip-Clop

I have a good mount this morning. They call her Mom. She's a gentle, steady horse. I wonder how many funerals like this she has been part of? She makes me think of my

Mom, gentle and steady, always there. Even when I decided to re-up in the Army.

Clip-Clop. Clip-Clop.

I didn't mean to, but I got a glimpse of the family while the casket was being placed on the caisson. Two older couples. Parents I suppose. A young woman —wife? And a small boy about six or seven. I wonder if he really understands what is happening here. Perhaps one day he will. They are following along quietly behind the caisson now.

Clip-Clop. Clip-Clop.

Almost at the grave site. There's the Casket Team waiting for us. Be sure to hold the horses steady while they lift the casket off the caisson. There, that's done. Wait a bit while the team and the family walk to the grave site.

They're gone now. Time for us to leave.

Yes, she thought, *this is a privilege and I can do it. But why must there be so many funerals. .*

Clip-Clop. Clip-Clop.

HELLO, HELLO

Hello, hello? Earth can you hear me? This is God calling. Yes, that God. I thought it was time we had a talk.

I'm calling to tell you that I am really pissed off at all, well, almost all, of you.

Look, I gave you this lovely planet and what 'ave you done with it: you've polluted the air, cut down acres and acres of trees, filled most of its rivers with toxic runoffs. And now your f_ _ _ _ing up the oceans with tons and tons of plastic garbage.

I put lots of beautiful animals down there for you to share the earth with and you are driving them into extinction faster than I can create them. Whales, elephants, polar bears...you are killing them off as if you hated them. That was not the plan.

I gave you Beethoven, Einstein, Rembrandt, Da Vinci, Shakespeare and Winston Churchill to occupy your minds and you developed Punk Rock and Donald Trump! Is that really the best you can do?

Listen Earth, it's been a while since I've done anything really radical but I still know how to cause a flood if I choose to. And this time there will be no Noah — so don't make me come down there.

Shape-up Earth or it will really be goodbye for you.

I will not call you a second time.

Goodbye.

SAY WHAT?

"Honey, do you believe in love at first sight?"

Pause...

More pause...

"Honey, I asked you..."

"I heard you. I know what you asked. This is a difficult question. Give me a moment to collect my thoughts."

"Oh sure, O.K."

Pause...

Alfred Gibbs loved his cars so, no, I guess I don't believe in love at first sight."

"Thanks for that answer. It helps to know where you stand on such an important question."

Pause...

"Err Hon, I appreciate your answer but I'm a bit confused. Can you tell me what Alfred Gibbs has to do with your opinion about love at first sight?"

"Well when you asked me if I believed in love at first sight my first thought was compared to what? As compared, for example, to Jimmy Cook? I didn't think much of Jimmy Cook until after my second or third look. And then he started to look pretty good to me. But then he took over his fathers undertaking business which meant he spent a lot of time with dead people and after that he didn't laugh much because it was bad for business. And then I though They say laughter is food for the soul. And poor jimmy's soul must have been starving to death. And I don't want to starve to death. You know how much I love pasta Alfredo. So, then I though, Maybe a comparison to Alfred Gibbs would be better. But Alfred really loved cars more than anything else. But he only loved the cars that he fixed up and modified himself. So, as handsome as he was, it's a good thing I didn't let that first sight of Alfred Gibbs overwhelm me because I certainly would not want the likes of Alfred Gibbs, or anyone else, fixing me up and modifying me so, no, I guess I don't believe in love at first sight.

Oh, O.K.. Now I understand. Thanks Hon."

KEEPING OUT OF TROUBLE

March 5, 1972,

New York City Police Department,

Central Park Station.

"You sent for me Captain?"

"Yeah, come on in Vince. Shut the door and have a seat."

The patrolman took a seat opposite the captain's desk.

"Personnel has reminded me that you're due for retirement in November," the captain said.

"Yes sir, it's been thirty years, and I've reached the mandatory retirement age. So I guess I'll have to be leaving," the patrolman replied.

"Got any plans?"

"Yes, sir. I've bought a farm upstate near Albany. It's a beautiful place, one hundred and twenty acres. It's got an old house on it that I can work on and a tractor."

"But you've been a city cop for most of your life. Do you know anything about farming?"

"No," the patrolman answered, "but hay grows naturally on the place so I'll mow it down with the tractor and then give it away to my neighbors."

"If I remember correctly you've got two sons haven't you," the captain inquired. "How are they doing? Are they going to work the farm with you?"

"They're doing fine. One is a firefighter here in the city. The other is an architect in Washington D.C. I'm sure they'll visit me on the farm and spend some time when they can."

"Sounds like you've got as nice retirement set up for yourself. Now Vince, you probably know why I've asked you to see me but let me spell it out for you so there will be no misunderstanding. Everyone here in the precinct is rooting for you to get to that retirement in November.

That means we want you to stay out of trouble for the next nine months. So here's what I'm going to do. I'm going to assign you to a patrol car. In it, you will have a radio so you can hear everything that's going on in our district. I, no, we, expect you to use that radio to stay away from any dangerous situations. Got it?"

"Yes sir, stay away from trouble. I've got it. Thank you, sir."

September 13, 1972,

three months to retirement.

1:30 a.m.

"Dispatch, this is car 92. Run a plate for me New York HJ22789. White, late model Jaguar sedan."

Moments later Dispatch answered "92, dispatch. HJ22789 a white 1971 Jaguar sedan is reported as a stolen vehicle."

92," Dispatch I am lighting it up and will attempt to interrogate. Uh oh, he;s taking off. I'm in pursuit. Westbound towards the Triborough Bridge".

Dispatch, "All units in the vicinity of the Triborough Bridge assist unit 92."

Car 103, "103 responding."

Car 68," 68 responding."

92, " We are entering the Triborough bridge going toward Manhattan"

92:,"Exiting the Triborough. Heading South on FDR Drive".

68, "Dispatch 68, I have eyes on 92. Am following."

103, "Dispatch, 103. I am just crossing the Triborough. Will continue the pursuit."

92, " Exiting the FDR heading West on 116 Street."

Patrolman Vince, in his patrol car, was located at 73rd Street and Central Park West. He had been following the car chase on his radio. Oh, Damn! He thought He'sheading my way. I'll go back to 72nd St. and go east through Central Park.

In the offices of the New York Daily News: in the Radio dispatch room Agnes Roberts, the evening dispatcher, has been listening to the car chase on her police scanner. She radioed to Mike Wilson a staff reporter, "Mike, are you listening to this car chase on the Upper East Side?"

"Yeah."

"Where are you right now," Agnes asked

"I'm at 38th Street and 7th Avenue."

"That's the Atomic Bar and Grill. Finish your beer and get up to Central Park and see if you can pick up that car chase and stay with it. Get a photo if you can. Let me know if you get anything."

"Okay, I'm on it, but you owe me a beer." He exited the Atomic Bar and Grill and headed towards Central Park. He continued to follow the car chase on his police scanner.

92, "Turning south on Central Park West."

92, " There seems to be just one male occupant in the Jaguar. Now he's cut into the Park at 97th Street. Heading East."

East. Now he's heading east. Patrolman Vince thought to himself. Okay, as soon as I exit the park I'll make a U-turn and go back West. Gotta stay out of trouble just like the Captain said.

103, " I'm going south on Fifth Avenue. Might be able to cut him off."

Dispatch, "10 . 4"

103, " I see him coming out of the park. He's turning south on Fifth Avenue. I'm in pursuit."

Patrolman Vince exited the park, made a U-turn and headed back through Central Park at 72nd St. going west.

103," Cutting back through the park at 79th Street."

103, " Going South on Central Park West."

103, " He's bumped another car on 77th Street."

103, " Back into the park at 72nd Street. Going East.

"Oh shit," Patrolman Vince said out loud. "There he is, and he's coming straight at me.

The car thief saw patrolman Vince's car straight ahead. In a desperate move, he veered the Jaguar off the road and headed toward Central Park Lake. On the way, he smashed into a park bench, lost control of the Jaguar and banged up against the knee-high wall that surrounds the lake. He exited the car, stepped over the wall and started to wade out toward the middle of the lake.

Patrolman Vince saw no choice but to follow the thief into the lake. Policemen from cars 103, 92 and 68 are close behind. Vince is the first to reach the thief— he tackled him, and both went tumbling into the knee deep water. The other officers quickly took charge of the suspect, but Patrolman Vince was credited with the "collar".

September 14, 1972. The New York Daily News, page two showed a photograph of a policeman and the car thief standing knee deep in Central Park Lake. The suspect was in handcuffs. The caption under the photo read: Patrolman Vincent Conway is shown holding Mark Edgerton, a car thief, who was captured in Central Park following last night's high-speed auto chase on the Upper East Side.

HOW TO GET TO RUSSIA
FROM ALASKA

The distance isn't great, less than 70 miles, and the ambitious traveler has several options such as:

- When the weather is right you could walk there.
- When the weather is right you could drive there
- You could swim there if swimming is your thing
- You might get there on a fishing boat if you are lucky enough to catch one.
- From time-to-time cruise ships go there.
- Commercial airlines fly there
- Private planes can make the trip in about sixty minutes
- A hearty cross-country skier could make the trip
- You could get there by dog sled, either your own or with one for hire.

So you see going from Alaska to Russia across the Bering sea is not an impossible trip. You will, no doubt, be traveling from Wales, Alaska (about 50 miles below the Arctic Circle) with a stop at Little Diomede island, the Westernmost point in the USA followed by a stop at Big Diamonde island the Easternmost point in Russian, Siberia. Your stop on Littlie Diomede island will probably be brief but you will find the 110 Ingalikmiut Eskimo inhabitants to be happy to greet their fellow Americans (or anyone else for that matter.)

Thanks to Wikipedia we can present the following overview of Little Diomede to assist you in planning your trip.

Weather: Summer temperatures average 40 to 50 degrees, winter from -10 to 6 Fahrenheit. Annual precipitation is 10 inches of rainfall, with 30 inches of snowfall.

Historical Overview Little Diomede island has been home to a small number of Ingalikmiut Eskimos for centuries. The island was named by Russian explorer Vitus Bering on St. Diomede's Day, August 16, 1728.

During WWII, Big Diomede served as a Russian military base. All residents were removed to the mainland and any Little Diomede inhabitants who strayed across the waters too close to Big Diomede were taken captive by the Russians.

After WWII the two island communities, connected by Eskimo family kinships but separated by American/Russian politics, led parallel lives — pictures of Karl Marx hung in the Russian schools, pictures of Abraham Lincoln in the American. Little Diomede villagers watched Warner Bros. films, Big Diomede watched movies made by Lenfilm.

True to Soviet tradition, Big Diomede Eskimos attempted to proselytize their Little Diomede relatives. "Come across the water," they are reported as urging. "Here we Eskimos are allowed to lubricate machines, cure the sick, write letters, live with Russian women, spit on merchants, go to Moscow."

Economy Little Diomede Eskimos live a subsistence lifestyle, harvesting fish and crab, hunting beluga whales, walrus, seals and polar bears. Almost every part of the animal is used for food, for clothing, mukluks, even boats. Locals are known for their ivory carving.

A few residents work for the local government or school. There has been some commercial fishing and mining on the island, but both industries are in decline.

The limited terrain does not allow for a runway, so weekly mail delivery is made by helicopter. Float planes rarely risk landing on the rough seas in summer, but ski planes do occasionally land on an ice runway during the winter months. Most supplies come from an annual barge delivery. The sale and importation of alcohol are banned.

You should be aware that Little Diomede island sits directly East of the International Dateline. This means that when you travel the two miles West from Little Diomede island (USA) to your next stop, Big Diomede island (Russia) you will gain one day on your calendar i.e. 9:00a.m on Sunday, August the 1st will become 9:00 a.m.

Monday, August 2nd. Not to worry however since on your return trip from West to East you will lose a day (which raises the interesting question as to whether or not you could return to your childhood if you traveled from West to East ad infinitum. Think about it.)

It is only if you continue to travel Westward once you get to Russia, will you be a day ahead of yourself forever.

Assuming you have seen enough of Little Diomede island you may now cross the border between the USA and Russia and arrive at Big Diomede island.

Welcome to Russia...providing your paperwork is in order. Here is what you need to know: Big Diomede island is in an autonomous district of Russian, Siberia known as Чукотка, (*choo-KOHT-kuh*). Entry into this district is limited – even to Russian citizens– and requires a special permit called a propusk. To enter Russia you will need a valid U.S. passport, a Russian entry visa, and a propusk. Contact your local Russian Consulate and expect to wait from nine to twenty weeks for your documents.

Having run the gauntlet of Russian bureaucracy we can now tell you a bit about Big Dolomede island, again, thanks to Wikipedia.

History The island was originally inhabited by Inupiat Eskimos sometime in the distant past.

The first European to reach the islands was the Russian explorer Semyon Dezhnyov in 1648. The Danish navigator (in Russian service) Vitus Bering re-discovered the Diomede Islands on August 16, 1728, the day on which the Russian Orthodox Church celebrates the memory of the martyr St. Diomede.

In 1867, during the Alaska Purchase, the new border between the nations was drawn between the Big Diomede and Little Diomede islands.

20th century During World War II, Big Diomede became a military base and remained so for some time into the Cold War.

After World War II, the native population was forced off Big Diomede Island to the mainland to avoid contacts across the border. Today, unlike Alaska's neighboring

Little Diomede Island, it has no permanent native population, but it is the site of a Russian weather station and a base of Russian Border Guard troops.

During the Cold War, the section of the border between the USA and the USSR separating Big and Little Diomede islands became known as the "Ice Curtain". In 1987, however, Lynne Cox swam from Little Diomede to Big Diomede (approx. 2.2 miles) and was congratulated jointly by Mikhail Gorbachev and Ronald Reagan.

Having arrived at Big Dolomede island you will, no doubt, be greeted by the some-times-friendly and sometimes-not-so friendly Russian Border Guards. The tenor of your welcome will be directly proportional to all of the above-mentioned documents being acceptable to the Russian peasant soldier who examines them plus the number of cigarettes, bottles of Scotch and American money you are prepared to part with as a gesture of friendship to our Russian neighbors.

Once again, we are thankful to Wikipedia for the following: Your stay on Big Dolomede island will be short and you will soon be on your way to either a Russian Gulag or the city of Provideniya (pop 2500 plus a large number of Polar Bears.)

Providenia is located on the northeast edge of Chukotka and is approximately one hour from Nome Alaska. This region, though not filled with shopping or city entertainment, is an unforgettable retreat. Coming into Provideniya will take visitors to a deep-water port that is surrounded by treeless mountains and is populated by a blend of cultures including Russian, Chukchi, and Siberian Chukchi. When in town, guests can go to Emma Bay for bird watching, or tour the Museum of Chukotcka history.

Travelers should be aware that there are no roads or trains out of Provideniya. The occasional small airplane is the only means for traveling into the nether regions of Siberia.

You have now reached the end of the world.

This writer recommends that once you have completed your tour of the Museum of Chukotchka history, before you are eaten by a polar bear, and before you freeze you're a _ _ off, you immediately start your return trip to Alaska.

This completes our discussion of How to go from Alaska to Russia and why you wouldn't want to go there.

BADGE 18611

Every member of the New York City Police Department (NYPD) is given a badge with a number. The badge number is the officer's primary identification with the NYPD. Detective Harry Eginton's badge number was 18611. His assignment was with the Vice Squad covering the Times Square district which included 7th Ave to Park Avenue and 38th Street to 59th Street. In 1964, it was the highest area for vice crime in the city. Prostitution (male and female), drug sales and use (any doorway was convenient.) public drunkenness and urination and the occasional sex act in public were the daily fares in the district.

Harry was a good cop. He understood that a number of the prostitutes had families to support and for those he used a 10 to 1 ratio; Ten tricks allowed then 1 arrest. The professional "working girls" in the district knew the rules and when it came to their turn to be picked up they simply chalked it up to the cost of doing business. There was never any violence and they always asked, "How are the kids Harry?"

Drug dealers were something else. Detective Eginton hated them with a passion. When arrested, drug pushers always seemed to suffer a "fall" resulting in injuries of one sort or another.

In their occasional conversations, Harry always explained to the "working girls" that he was actually trying to protect them from the drug pushers. "There are enough hazards to your business," he would explain. "You don't need a drug problem as well." Most of the women appreciated his advice even if they didn't all follow it. But Gracie and Doris were the exceptions. Both had children to support. All they wanted to do was get on with their work and then get home to the kids. Not only Did Gracie and Doris listen to detective Eginton's advice they rather looked for him to be their protector out on the street. It could be a violent place and having Harry to watch your back was a good feeling.

All in all, it was an amicable working arrangement for everyone. Harry got his quota of arrests and Gracie and Doris were not abused.

The drug dealers had different thoughts about Harry. They were feeling the pressure of his arrests and confiscation of their products. They had to do something about Detective Eginton and Evelyn fit the bill perfectly.

To begin with, Evelyn's territory was in Brooklyn so she was not known by any of the working girls in the Times Square district. Secondly, Evelyn had a one hundred dollar a day heroin habit. The drug dealers wanted her to set Harry up for a sex crime. If she pulled this off, and if Harry was taken off the Times Square Vice Squad, Evelyn would be supplied with heroin for a year. The risk to Evelyn was that she might have to serve some time in the Women's Detention Center but that was not a problem, the dealers would see to it that she got her drugs even while in jail. Evelyn agreed to the deal.

The plan was for Evelyn to come to Manhattan and work the area around 37th Street and 7th Avenue. They knew that eventually Harry would pick her up and that was when they would spring the trap. Once Harry had her in his unmarked police car, an anonymous complaint would be called in to the police station about a man and a woman engaged in sex acts in a car parked on 37th Street.

The plan was put into operation and Evelyn started working the streets. Like all good business women Gracie and Doris wanted to find out about this new competition. Instinctively they did not like Evelyn and both agreed that something was "fishy" about this broad. They agreed to keep an eye on her.

They also expressed their suspicions to detective Harry. He observed Evelyn for a week and came to the same conclusion...something was not right with her. She was too conspicuous in her sexy costume and too open and obvious in her solicitations of the "Johns." Harry decided to have a talk with her. He picked her up one evening around midnight. Gracie and Doris were nearby and waited around to see what would happen. The spotter for the drug dealers was also watching.

As soon as Evelyn got into Harry's car the spotter made an anonymous call to the police precinct, lectured the desk sergeant about immorality on the streets of New York and hung up.

Out of curiosity, Gracie and Doris walked over to Harry's car to get a better look at what was going on.

Within four minutes marked police cars entered 37th Street from each end.

"This don't look right," Gracie said.

"I think Harry is in some kind of trouble," Doris rasped. She pulled open the rear door of the car, jumped in, and pulled Gracie in after her.

The three women were arrested, Harry was relieved of his service revolver, and everyone was taken to the police station for interviews.

Evelyn's story was that Harry had been shaking her down for money and sexual favors for the past week.

Harry, of course, denied all of it. Gracie and Doris insisted that all three women were in Harry's car on a routine arrest for prostitution and that Evelyn's story was not true. Once she was faced with Gracie and Doris' version of the incident, Evelyn broke down and confessed all about the drug dealers plot.

At the trial, Gracie and Doris testified on Harry's behalf and the judge accepted their story. Harry was reinstated to duty with the Vice Squad. Evelyn, Gracie, and Doris were sentenced to six months in the Women's Detention Center. While there, Evelyn suffered a "fall" with multiple injuries.

TIME FOR A

KAISERSCHMARREN

(Kaiser-schmar-ren)

The crowd of Japanese tourists rushed across the Stephanplatz toward the massive doors of St. Stephan's cathedral. Not even the heat of Vienna on this lovely June day could slow them down—after all, there were photos to be taken—and the 14th Century cathedral beckoned.

As for me, I hold fast to my "viewing point." And now, dear reader, I will share the secret of my viewing point with you. If you go to Austria, and if you go to Vienna and, if you go to the Stephan Platz, the very heart of Vienna, and walk to a spot about 120 feet directly in front of the main doors of the cathedral you will find a cast iron manhole cover embedded in the pavement. You will know you are at the right place because the manhole cover—itself a work of art—is beautifully embossed with the crest and words "Vienna Department of Sewer Works"

Now that you are standing on the viewing point, here is what you must do: raise your eyes and, starting at the great doors of the cathedral, slowly, very, very slowly make a 360 degree turn and allow your eyes and brain to record a panorama of the loveliness of the world's most elegant city.

Your eyes will observe several high-end pedestrian shopping streets that empty into the Stephanplatz. You are bound to see several horse-drawn carriages as they pass the high fashion shops. There will be chocolateries with an aroma that will make your mouth water, a Wienerwald restaurant, the Hotel Am Stephanplatz, a shop for traditional Austrian clothing such as the famous Loden coats and capes, and of course, you will see Schuetz's Konditorei (the home of world class pastries). No doubt you will want to linger over the luscious display of cakes, pies and torte but you must move on to complete your panorama. Finally your vision will bring you back to the main doors of the Cathedral.

Having securely locked this glorious panorama in your mind, months or even years afterwards, you can recall it and savor the beauty of Vienna.

Now it is time to retreat to Schuetz's Konditori for a cup of the wonder that is Viennese coffee and a Kaiserschmarren*

*A Viennese desert served with raspberry sauce and powdered sugar. It is not to be missed when you visit this romantic city.

EYEWITNESS

First Eyewitness (FEW): I couldn't help noticing her when she came into Panera's. Such an attractive young woman.

Second Eyewitness (SEW): What a mess. I thought. No make-up, Sweaty jogging shorts, and sneakers that had seen better days.

Third Eyewitness (TEW): Nice bod, short hair all windblown. Looks like a high-class lawyer out for her morning run.

FEW: She stopped just inside the entrance and scanned the tables, obviously looking for someone.

SEW She seemed to know exactly what table he would be sitting at and she headed straight for it.

TEW: She spotted him right away but hesitated as if deciding whether or not she was going to go to him.

FEW: Once she spotted him she stormed over to the table and sat down in a huff.

SEW: She stopped beside the table, looked down at him, and placed her hand on his shoulder.

TEW: She stood back a bit from the table, and seemed to say a greeting. He looked up.

FEW: He turned off his iPad and waited for her to speak.

SEW: He closed the book he had been reading and smiled at her.

TEW: He seemed surprised to see her. He had been deeply engrossed in the Magazine Section of The New York Times.

FEW: Clearly she was angry at him. She almost spat out her first words.

SEW: She smiled back and took her seat opposite him. They seemed happy to see each other.

TEW: He closed the paper he had been reading and, with a gesture, invited her to have a seat. They clasped hands across the table and looked into each other's eyes.

FEW: He tried to respond to her angry words but she cut him short. Then she grabbed his water glass and threw the water in his face.

SEW: At the next moment she started to cry, all the while, shaking her head no.

TEW: His face and posture took on a downcast look. He seemed to be apologizing for something.

FEW: Without another word she rose and stormed out of the restaurant.

SEW: He was speaking rapidly to her now as if he was trying to convince her of something. She tore her hands away from his and ran sobbing from the restaurant.

TEW: She shook her head in an understanding way. Then she reached across the table and stroked his cheek. They rose together and left the restaurant arm-in-arm.

GIDDYAP JOHNSON

"Basta, enough!" Benny the Tailor cried as he threw a copy of the Daily Racing Form on the table. "I can't make no sense outta dese picks in today's races. One handicapper says 'Can-do is the horse to go with', an dis udda guy says 'Catzanova is a sure ting at seven ta five', an' somebody else says 'Green Dude could win if the track is muddy' A person couldn't even make a decent living wid dat kinda advice."

"I know, I know," chimed in Bam Bam De Luca. "I fell into a hunnert clams, and I can't find no horse I like either. I don't know what dis country is comin' to when a guy can't pick up some easy scratch at da track no more."

"Ya see, ya see, dat's just what I been telling youse guys," Jerry Johnson said. "It's like this guy Karl Marx sez, 'Ya gotta own da means of production.' For years now we been bettin' on the end result of races. Da way to make a killin' is ya gotta own da horse, 'cause da horse is da means of production. Dat's where da real dough is. So dat's why I am gonna buy a race horse."

"Whaaat!" sez Benny the tailor.

"You must be crazy," Bam Bam de Luca observes. "Youse don't know nothin' about horses."

"What's to know?" Jerry answered. "All ya gotta do is get on 'em and say giddyap and if da horse is fast he wins and youse take da money to the bank."

"Yeah but what about training 'em, and feeding 'em, and all dat stuff?"

"I don't have to worry about dat stuff. The guy I'm buyin' dis horse from knows all about dat, an' he's gonna stay on as my trainer."

"Ownin' a horse costs a lot of money. Where'd you get dat kinda dough?"

"Let's just say I got a midnight loan from a Chase Bank branch when I made dat trip to Cincinnatti. So now, like Marx says, I'm gonna own da means of production. As for youse guys, if youse can't make up your minds about today's races, maybe it's time to go see Moe the Jew."

Moe the Jew is an honored, highly respected, and unique institution on the street. To begin with, he is an old-fashioned, dapper-looking guy who, in this day and age, still wears spats and a Homburg hat. He is a handicapper who makes his living off the horses, or to put it more correctly, he makes his living off guys who play the horses.

In all his seventy-odd years Moe the Jew has never placed a bet on a horse, but he has studied horses for most of those seventy years. Moe can tell you all the statistics on every horse that has run a race for the past ten years. He knows who their parents were, how much every jockey weighs, when the horse was last seen by a vet, and why. Moe can probably tell you what every horse had for breakfast today.

So when horse players get stuck and can't figure out which horse to bet on, they go to Moe for his picks of the day. Now, he's is not always right ... but he is right much more often than he is wrong.

On the street the unwritten rule is that if Moe the Jew picks a winner for you, he gets ten percent of the winnings. This is how Moe, and his friend Nuch, make their living. Not that Nuch is a handicapper, far from it. His name comes from the Yiddish word nuchshlepper, which, loosely translated, means "hanger-on". He is not very bright. Speculation on the street is that he has the I.Q. of a basset hound, which makes him the perfect "gofer" and companion for Moe. Wherever Moe goes, Nuch follows.

Over the years every one of the hundred or so serious horse players on the street has gone to Moe. In the end they have all made money off his tips. Their aggregate winnings probably come close to seven figures.

Jerry Johnson bought his racehorse. He named it "Wiseguy". In his first three races, Wiseguy finished in the middle of the pack and did not earn any money. The citizens of the street watched and waited for Wiseguy to start winning. They waited, and waited, and waited. Jerry Johnson took a lot of ribbing from one and all. A current joke on the street was to walk past Jerry and say, "Giddyap, giddyap." By the end of the second racing season, Jerry was simply known as "Giddyap Johnson".

One day, when things on the street were very quiet, a bunch of the guys were hanging around Little Augie Martorano's office, aka the back room of the Villa Napoli Restaurant aka the headquarters of the Martorano Mafia Family. In walks Nuch for his afternoon plate of veal scaloppini. Nuch is looking very sad, indeed. When asked, "What's up," he replied, "It's Moe the Jew. He's had a stroke. He's an old man, ya know."

This is heavy news, and the word quickly spreads around the street of the old man's misfortune. The word gets out that Moe is in a nursing home called The Peaceful Palace. Nuch, of course, visits him every day, and then reports to all interested parties on Moe's condition.

It turns out that the Peaceful Palace is a very expensive place, and Nuch does not know how much longer Moe can stay there. The looming alternative is the charity ward at the county hospital. This is very distressing news to Little Augie who, like everyone else, has benefited from Moe's advice over the years. So Little Augie calls for a meeting for one and all to come and talk about Moe's situation.

The room was filled with maybe ninety or a hundred people. A number of ideas were tossed out and discussed but none really caught on. Finally, Giddyap Johnson stood up and said as follows, "Youse all know I have dis horse named Wiseguy, who is not doing so good at the track. It is also true dat dis horse is costing me an arm and a leg to maintain, and I would not mind gettin' out from under him. Now, I know a guy who can mix up a cocktail that would make Wiseguy a sure winner in the third race at Belmont Park next Thursday. With his record, the odds against Wiseguy will be around thirteen to one. Now, if everyone in this room was to bet on Wiseguy ...."

The following Friday Nuch deposited a very very large check with the Peaceful Palace, thereby guaranteeing Moe the Jew a comfortable future for many years to come.

Wiseguy died of a heart attack two days later and Giddyap Johnson became a hero all up and down the street and around and about.

LITTLE AUGIE

This is the story of how Little Augie Martorano became the Capo de Familia of the Martorano Mafia family of Brooklyn, New York.

The first thing you have to understand is how names are handled in Italian families. If a male child is born and is named Augustus, which is a very popular name in Italian families, then that child will grow up being known as Little Augie. If a second child is born into the extended family, say a cousin, who is also named Augustus, then the second child will be known as Big Augie. The logic of this is that the second is a larger number than the first hence he is bigger. Capisce?

So in the Martorano family we have two Augies, Little Augie and Big Augie. Now even though these cousins share the same name they turn out to be very different people. Little Augie takes a serious interest in the family business while Big Augie turns out to be a straight, stand-up kind of guy who even takes a stupid job with the New York Port Authority, collecting tolls at the Holland tunnel. This, of course, is something of a disgrace to the Martorano family but hey, waddya gonna do wid kids?

The second thing you have to know about Mafia family names is that almost everyone has some kind of nickname...sort of a nom de alias. If you don't got a nickname fuhgeddaboutit; you get no respect from the family.

Now at the time of which I am speaking the Martorano Mafia family of Brooklyn, New York, is not one of your large Mafia families...though they are very respectable as Mafia families go. The Martoranos are putting the squeeze on twenty or thirty restaurants in their territory. In a brilliant move that would be called "vertical integration" in normal business circles, they also control all of the garbage trucks in their territory. Of course the twenty or thirty restaurants are filling these garbage trucks with free garbage which is sold to pig farmers across the river in Newark, New Jersey for a very handsome profit indeed. With this and various and sundry slightly illegal enterprises, the Martorano family is doing okay. But like any business, they have got problems.

In fact the Martoranos have got two problems. The first is with the old Capo Familia, Little Aggie's father. It's clear to one and all in the family that the old capo is loosing his marbles. There is even a rumor that he has this here wadda call it..."Al Heimers disease."

The second problem the Martorano's have got is with the Costa family. The Costas have got big eyes for the Martorano's territory and for the past year or so they have been trying to muscle their way into it.

So, like all good families what has got problems, the Martoranos call a meet-up to bring everyone to the table to discuss the situation. They even bring in the consigliere to advise them what they should do.

The two main contenders for the Capo Familia position are Benny the Taylor and The Roach, who has this name because he looks like a roach. Both of these contenders get great respect from the family because they have each whacked enough citizens to make a serious dent in the population of Brooklyn, New York. Little Augie, on the other hand, is just a young guy who has not yet had no opportunity to whack even one citizen. Still, as the old capo's only son, everyone admits that he has a legitimate claim to the position.

At the family meet-up Little Augie stands up and says as follows, "Wid all due respect to Benny the Taylor and the Roach I am, as youse know, a graduate from Erasmus Hall High School. As such I think I have got the brain power to out smart the Costa family. Therefore, I deserve to be the capo of this here family. If youse will give me six months, I will prove this to youse"

The consigliare figures this is a fair proposition, and Little Augie gets his six months.

Now, being a graduate from Erasmus Hall High School, Little Augie is a very smart cookie, indeed. He has seen from as much as a year ago what is going on with the

Costa family. So to give him an ace in the hole, Little Augie has planted a ratfink inside the Costa family. He figures that with the information the ratfink is passing on to him, he will be able to outsmart the Costas.

His first opportunity comes when the ratfink tells him about a heist the Costas are going to pull on the Brooklyn docks. It seems that a ship has just arrived with a load of very expensive Argentine beef. The word on the street is that a truckload of this beef is worth a cool two hundred thousand large.

The Alabama Beef Packing Company has sent an eighteen-wheeler truck, driven by a local hick, to pick up the beef. This driver turns out to be such a hick, and so unfamiliar with the ways of New York City, that the night before he is to pick up the beef he has a tragic accident and falls off the Brooklyn Bridge while in the company of two gorillas from the Costa family. So all that is needed now is for the Costa's to send their own driver to the docks to pick up the beef. And who do the Costas pick to do this but Joey Bananas!

It is generally agreed far and wide and around and about that Joey Bananas deserves this name. Everyone knows that Joey is not the brightest banana in the bunch. In fact, Joey Bananas is an ex-prizefighter who has been punched in the head so many times that his brain now looks like a bowl of oatmeal. If youse want some muscle put on a guy or if youse want some shoe leather applied to someone's face, Joey Bananas is your boy. But if you got a job that requires some brain power... fuhgeddaboudit–Joey is the last person youse would pick.

On the day of the heist Joey Bananas is sitting in the cab of the eighteen-wheeler getting ready to drive off with the beef when around the corner comes a guy in a green uniform. On the shoulder of this guy's jacket is a patch that says "United States Department of Agriculture." This guy is wearing a name tag that says "Beef Inspector," and he is carrying a small case that has "U.S. Department of Agriculture Official Beef Inspection Kit" written on it.

The beef inspector walks up to Joey Bananas and says like this: "Youse cannot leave these docks without first I gotta inspect this beef"

Now this is very confusing to Joey Bananas, because nobody has said nothing to him about no beef inspector. Joey figures he has two choices. Either he can whack this guy right now or he can let him inspect the beef. On second thought, Joey figures that if he whacks this guy it will probably bring the U.S. Air Force or the CIA or the Smithsonian Institution down on the Costa family, which would not be a good thing. So Joey tells the inspector to, "Go ahead and inspect the beef."

The inspector goes around to the back of the truck and climbs in. About five minutes later, he comes out holding a dead cat.

"This beef is poisoned and I am impounding this truck forthwith. Also," he says, "since youse have been sitting in this truck for some time now the poison has probably seeped out from the back of this truck and is maybe killing you as we speak. If I was youse, I would get to a hospital right away and have myself checked out. Youse may be dying at this very minute."

This kind of talk throws Joey Bananas into a total panic, Since he figures the poisoned beef is no good to the Costas anyhow, he takes a powder at high speed and he runs off looking for a hospital.

No sooner does Joey get out of sight then Little Augie whips off the green cap and jacket and, badda bing, badda boom, he drives off with the beef.

It is not long after this that we hear that Joey Bananas has suffered a tragic accident and has fallen off the Brooklyn Bridge.

At the next meet-up of the Martorano family, Benny the Taylor and The Roach have got to admit the Little Augie has done good, especially since the Argentine beef actually sells for the two hundred thousand large. Once again, Little Augie stands up and says as follows, "Youse ain't seen nothin' yet. I am just getting started wid the Costas, and I still have five months to go."

His next chance comes when the ratfink tells him of a fixed horse race at Belmont Park that the Costas are planning to tap into. Here's how it comes about. The capofamilia of the Costa family has a daughter named Angelina, who youse would know as Angie. Angie is married to a guy named "No Shadow DePalma." He is called this because he is such a skinny runt of a guy that he does not even cast a shadow on the ground. For such a guy, there is only one possible kind of job, which is as a horse jockey.

No Shadow DePalma is scheduled to ride in the fifth race at Belmont Park next week. This race maybe, is going to be fixed. Entered in this race is a horse called "Paul Revere." He is such a dog of a horse that if there was a race between him and his jockey, the jockey would win by two furlongs. In fact he is such a dog the odds against him in the race are twelve to one. The owner figures to shoot the horse up with such a potent cocktail that he will make a champion such as Man O' War look like he is standing still. To be sure that nobody catches on to the scheme the owner has to wait until the very last minute before doctoring up the horse.

No Shadow DePalma arranged two signals to let the Costas know whether or not the fix is on. If the fix is on, No Shadow will adjust his helmet as the horses are paraded to the starting gate. If the owner has not been able to doctor up the horse, No Shadow will scratch his boot on the way to the starting gate in which case the Costas will not place no bets.

On the day of the race, No Shadow DePalma does not notice that there is a new attendant in the jockey's locker room. This is because the old attendant, just last night, suffered a tragic accident and fell off the Brooklyn Bridge while in the company of two gorillas from the Martorano family. So while No Shadow DePalma is in the shower the new attendant fills his boots with itching powder. On the way to the starting gate No Shadow is scratching his boot like crazy which the Costas take as the signal that the race has not been fixed. They hold on to their money and go home.

The Martoranos, meantime, bet the entire two hundred thousand large on Paul Revere at thirteen to one. This is a no-risk bet for the Martoranos, since the two hundred thou is Costa money,, anyway. Paul Revere wins by two lengths, and the Martoranos make a killing...figuratively speaking, of course.

Not long after this the word is on the street that Angie is looking for a new husband ever since No Shadow DePalma suffers a tragic accident when he falls off the Brooklyn Bridge.

At the next meet-up of the Martorano family Benny the Taylor and The Roach are about ready to concede the Capo Familia position to Little Augie when he addresses the family as follows, "To give youse final proof that I deserve to be the capo I am going to administer the cup-de-grace to the Costa family. Next week I am going to steal two million dollars from the Costa family."

Now this is very big talk indeed, since everyone knows that nobody has never stole so much as one thin dime offa the Costa family. Here is how Little Augie pulls it off.

The ratfink has told him that next week the Costas are going to New Jersey to appropriate a Brinks armored car that is carrying the two million in payroll cash.

A caper such as this is something the Costas are very good at. So we see that in the final act of this heist, The Baron and Bam Bam, two Costa gorillas, are dressed in Brinks uniforms and are driving the armored car to the safety of the Costa warehouse in Brooklyn. The reason they are wearing these uniforms is because the former owners are now lying face down in a ditch just outside of Sheboygan, New Jersey and will not need no uniforms whatsoever ever again.

If youse have ever driven to New York from New Jersey through the Holland tunnel, youse know that getting up to a tollbooth is like a scene from Dante's Inferno, what with twelve lanes of cars trying to merge to five tollbooths. The Baron and Bam Bam enter the fray.

They do not notice that a large black Cadillac, which, by the way, the New York City Police Department has been looking for for two days, keeps nudging them toward tollbooth number three. Eventually, they get to the window. As Bam Bam is about to pay the toll, the man in the booth, who is none other than Big Augie, speaks like this, " I see from the license plate that this is a New Jersey vehicle and that, as is proper for Brinks guards, youse is packing heat. Please let me see your New York City gun registrations."

"What gun registrations?" sez Bam Bam

"The gun registrations what New York City Mayor Michael Bloomberg sez is required as of this morning."

"We ain't got no gun registrations," chimes in The Baron.

"Nobody gets into News York without they got a gun registration. I will tell youse what I will do," sez Big Augie. "Out of my high regard for the Brinks company I will hold up this line while youse go over there to the New York Port Authority office. There they will give youse your gun registrations. It will only take a minute and youse will be on your way."

So The Baron and Bam Bam get out of the armored car and start to make their way through twelve lanes of cars toward the office. No sooner do they get lost in the traffic than Little Augie jumps out of the big black Caddie, climbs into the Brinks truck, and drives off with the two million and his cousin Big Augie, who has suddenly decided on a career change even if it means giving up his pension from the New York Port Authority.

At the next meet-up of the Martorano family, Little Augie is voted in as the Capo Familia of the Martorano Mafia family of Brooklyn, New York.

It is not long after this that we hear of the tragic accident in which The Baron and Bam Bam fall off the Brooklyn Bridge.

A SISTERS LOVE

The small village of Bungoma, Kenya was both happy and sad. Happy because the wife of Kamau Nyakundi had just given birth to two beautiful twin girls. Sad because Kamau's wife did not survive the childbirth.

Never the less the girls, Adele and Adina, were cherished by the entire village and grew up being cared for and loved by everyone. In such a loving atmosphere, the bond between the twins grew stronger and stronger over the years. They were inseparable.

When, at last, Adele was married and gave birth to her own daughter. Adina, who lived with Adele and her husband, took to the child as if she were her own. It was as if Adele's daughter had been blessed with two loving and caring mothers.

In the normal course of a day, the twins shared the household chores; the most tedious of which was the fetching of water.

One day, when it was Adina turn to fetch the water, she decided to carry her infant niece along with her. Using a large cloth, she tied the baby to her back and started out for the well. She sang an ancient lullaby to the baby as she went along. Perhaps her singing attracted the attention of a hungry Cheetah.

When she arrived at the well, Adina laid the baby in the shade of a nearby tree while she filled the water jugs. The big cat sprang upon the little girl and immediately started to drag the body away. Adina grabbed the largest rock she could find and began to beat the Cheetah about its head all the while screaming and sobbing in panic as she tried to free the child. Not about to give up its prey, the cat turned on Adina, and with one swipe of its powerful claw knocked her to the ground where she fainted out of fear and panic. When she awoke, the Cheetah and her niece were gone.

Still, in a state of fear, panic, and remorse over the loss of her sister's child, she spent the next hour searching the nearby forest for some trace of the baby. To no avail. Eventually, in a kind of stupor over the realization of what had happened, she stumbled home.

It took Adele several weeks to work through the stages of grief over the loss of her child. When she finally managed to accept the tragedy, she turned her grief and anger against her sister. It became clear that Adina could no longer stay in the house. Heartbroken over the loss of both her sister and her niece she moved to a faraway village.

In the year that followed Adina's life was a maelstrom of grief, remorse and a bad decision, which she made to ally her feelings of guilt. Her bad decision was to marry a man who was unable to accept the responsibilities of married life. When Adina announced that she was pregnant he soon abandoned her and her newborn baby girl.

She got by as best she could. Then one day she developed a scheme that she felt certain would relieve her of her guilt over the loss of Adele's child.

For the next three years, she devoted herself to raising her own child as if she was her niece rather than her daughter. She went so far as to teach the child to address her as Auntie rather than Mother. At the end of the third year, she was ready to face her sister again.

She arrived at Adele house with the child in her arms.

Tearfully, and with the utmost contrition, Adina told her sister that she had come to confess her heinous crime. She told Adele that there had been no Cheetah attack but that out of envy and jealousy she had stolen Adele's daughter to raise as her own. But now, after all these years, Adina had come to regret her crime and was unable to go on living a false life. She had come to return Adele's daughter to her and beg for forgiveness. With this confession and cries of anguish, she handed her own daughter to Adele.

It took Adele several days to comprehend her sister's confession and to rejoice in the return of her lost child. When at last she absorbed the entire story and accepted her sister's remorse her childhood love for her sister overcame all other emotions and she welcomed Adina back into her home where the family lived in harmony for many years.

A BROTHERS LOVE

Benny Scadudo, Capo de Capo of the Scadudo Family, like most Sicilian men, was a proud father. And why not? Frankie, his twenty-one-year-old eldest son, was coming along nicely. He was taking an interest in the Family's businesses and he looked the way a prospective Capo should look. He had an olive complexion, dressed smartly and stayed away from drugs. Frankie was even taking classes at Brooklyn College.

On the other hand, Vinnie, his nineteen-year-old youngest son, left a bit to be desired. His interest in the Family's business was only cursory; baseball and basketball seemed to be his real passions. "But," Benny rationalized, "he's still a kid. He'll come around eventually." Vinnie had to be pushed to finish High School.

American Literature was a required course at Brooklyn College so Frankie took it not knowing what to expect. He got hooked. Steinbeck, Hemingway, O. Henry, Mark Twain opened up new worlds for Frankie and he couldn't get enough of it. The following semester he took a Creative Writing course and decided that his life's direction was set. He was going to be a writer. His father, Benny, would have none of it. "You're destined to become Capo de Capo of this family and that's all there is to it. End of Discussion."

Frankie begged, pleaded and argued with his father for two months. In a last-ditch attempt to keep his wayward son in the Family's business Benny agreed to support Frankie's writing efforts for two years. But there was a catch. If at the end of two years, no publisher had accepted any of Frankie's, work, then he was to give it up and come home and prepare to take over the Family. Frankie agreed. He took an apartment in Greenwich Village and started writing.

Benny was no fool and he was not a gambler. On the off chance that Frankie might succeed as a writer Benny turned his attention to grooming Vinnie for the top position. It wasn't easy to turn Vinnie's attention away from pro-sports so Benny started by letting him take-over the gambling portion of the Family business. It wasn't long before Vinnie came around and started assuming a role in the Family hierarchy. While Benny still held out hope that his oldest son would come back to the family he was satisfied that Vinnie, could inherit the Capo de Capo position if necessary.

Two years went by and Frankie came to the realization that he had no talent as a writer. The pile of rejection slips on his desk grew higher and higher. His father invoked their agreement, stopped all support for Frankie, and waited for him to return home. This was not to be. Frankie's exposure to the world of letters and life on a higher moral plane had changed him and his view of Mafia life. The thought of becoming part of it was anathema. There were several traumatic meetings with his father, who, in the pique of anger and frustration, disowned him and declared, "My son Frankie is dead to me. Now Vinnie is my only son."

Now on his own, Frankie drifted from job to job. Seven years after the separation from his father Frankie, now known simply as Frank Scadudo, was a Vice President, and Manager, of the Manhattan Branch of the Immigrant Savings bank on lower Broadway. Four armed men in ski masks entered the bank and announced that "This is a robbery. Do as we tell you and nobody will get hurt." Frank, seated in his office at the rear of the bank, understood at once what was happening. He was immediately outraged to think that this was happening at "his bank". In an irrational impulse, he drew a pistol from his desk draw thinking that he could frighten the robbers by firing several shots in their direction. One of his bullets struck the nearest bandit killing him instantly. His strategy worked, in that, the other robbers, seeing the body hit the floor, panicked and fled the scene.

When the police arrived and the pandemonium had calmed down the dead robber was unmasked. It was Vinnie.

That evening, Frank put a gun to his head, and pulled the trigger.

THE WORLD'S FIRST

ROBOT BABY

The BBC's (British Broadcasting Corporation) World News Service was sixteen minutes into it's 7:00PM news program. The news reader was reporting a story about Syrian refugees landing in Italy when a cameraman appeared on the set and handed the reader a sheet of paper. He stopped talking, read the paper and announced to the camera, "We interrupt this program to bring you a special bulletin." He read from the paper, "Computer scientists from the University of Glasgow, in Scotland, have just announced the worlds first birth by a robot. Their computer, UG806-A, affectionately known as Mrs. MacTavish, has just given birth to a fifteen pound offspring. Mother and baby are doing well."

The reader pressed a finger to the earpiece in his left ear, listened for a moment and then said, "My producer tells me that this is all the information we have about this remarkable story at the moment, but we will be following this earth shattering news throughout the evening."

The reader continued with the regular news broadcast. After a bit he announced that, "Following-up on the stunning news of the robot-human hybrid birth we now have Doctor Fergus MacDonald, the Director of the Robotics Laboratory at the University of Glasgow, on the line for an exclusive BBC interview about the remarkable event that took place at the university this evening. Doctor MacDonald can you hear me sir?"

Dr. MacDonald answered in a thick Scottish brogue, "Aye, I can hear ye."

BBC- "Doctor MacDonald what can you tell us about this amazing event, the world's first robot-human hybrid birth?"

Dr.M- "This birth is the result of fifteen years of work here at the University of Glasgow. It all began with the development of Mrs. MacTavish, officially the robot UG806-A. Slowly during all those years we were able to impart to her all the motherly instincts we were able to glean from the field of human psychology.

As time passed, and we monitored Mrs. Mactavish's memory chips, we found that she had come to realized there was something unusual about herself—something that made her different from all the other robots. There were mood changes, discomfort during sleep, back aches and increased hunger for computer chips and lug nuts. She could think of only one thing—she wanted a baby. She wanted a child to love, to mother, to teach. This was exactly the motherly instincts we had hoped she would develop. In other words, we had created a "Mother Robot".

At the same time that Mrs. MacTavish was developing her motherly instincts our engineers were able to program her with all the necessary steps to assemble a baby robot on her own, that is, without any human supervision or intervention. With increasing frequency she began to demonstrate motherly behaviors. We could tell that she was ready to give birth to her own baby. .After that, we simply enclosed her in a sealed environment with all the necessary components. We call this her gestation period. It took her four months to make her baby."

BBC- "That's remarkable — so you are saying that all on her own Mrs. MacTavish, your "Mother Robot" was able to create her own baby robot?"

Dr. M- "Aye, and we are pleased to announce that it's a baby boy. We have named him "The Wee Laddie.""

BBC- "Now wait just a minute, Doctor. We all know that machines, and robots are just machines, do not have genders as we humans do. How can you say that this baby is a boy?"

Dr. M- "What you say has been correct —until now.. What we have done is to pull together all the known personality characteristics of a human male and passed them, through Mrs. MacTavish, to The Wee Laddie. He will grow up to be as much a man as you or me."

BBC- "Truly amazing! But what do you mean when you say he will "grow up?"

Dr. M- "Well, of course, now he is just a wee bairn. He can see and hear, make sounds and move his arms and legs but over the next year or so Mrs. MacTavish will be given the necessary parts to give The Wee Laddie more memory, bigger and stronger arms and legs and so forth. It is our intention to help her see him through the stages of childhood, teenage, and into adulthood to the age of twenty-two or twenty-three years old."

BBC- "What will happen to him then?"

Dr. M- "We have already made arrangements for him to be employed at the Ford Motor plant here in Glasgow."

BBC- "What about Mrs. MacTavish? What will become of her?"

Dr. M- "Auch — we have great plans for her. Now that we have created a "Mother Robot" we will clone her. It is the University's wish that we create as many "Mother Robots" as we can. What's more, the University has decided to release all of her programs into the Public Domain. Now it will be possible for other universities, corporations or anyone else, to make their own "Mother Robots". We predict that in ten years there will be thousands of "Mother Robots" giving birth to hundreds of thousands of robot babies. The advantages to the human race will be phenomenal...we think.

BBC- "Thank you Doctor MacDonald. Unfortunately that is all the time we have just now, so this is the BBC saying... goodnight from London."

WAR STORIES AT THE VA

"Two eggs over medium and wheat toast," Vietnam said.

He took his eggs, toast, and coffee to the cashier. "Four twenty-seven Sweetie," she said and gave him his change. "Have a lovely day," she said.

In the dining area, he looked for a table. At first glance, they all seemed to be full but then he spotted one with three men, a woman, and an empty chair. "Mind if I join you?" he asked.

"Come on in Bro," Afghanistan said.

"And welcome to ya," Korea added

"I hope you were a Marine, " the woman said. "I hate being the only one here"

"Nope, Army," Vietnam answered.

"Airborne by any chance?" WWII queried.

"Just a Nam grunt," Vietnam answered.

"Vietnam, are you still on drugs?" The woman marine wanted to know.

"I never understood the drug thing," Korea said. "We were so busy freezing our asses off that the only thing we wanted was another pair of socks."

"Afghanistan never got below a hundred," Afghanistan said. "And since you never knew if a rag head or a woman in a burqa was going to blow you up we didn't dare try drugs."

"We were told that some of the Frenchies might try to do us in with poisoned wine," WWII said. "I volunteered to be the official taster for the entire Eighty-second Airborne. Sure drank a lot of wine between Normandy and Paris." He chuckled.

"In Korea, it was the women in black pajamas you had to watch out for. They would come towards you holding out a bowl of rice and when they got within thirty feet they would lob a grenade at your crotch."

"So what are we here at the VA for? The woman marine asked looking at everyone at the table.

New prosthetic leg," WWII answered

"Kidneys," Korea said. "I'm just getting old and starting to fall apart."

"I'm just here to pick up my Methadone," Vietnam said. "I've almost go it licked."

"It's called PTSD," Afghanistan said, looking around the table. "Bad dreams and fighting off suicide."

"Hang in there Bro," Vietnam said.

"We're all with you man," Korea said. "Here's my cell number. Call me anytime...and I mean anytime."

"Time is your best friend," WWII said. "You may not believe it now but take it from me. If you can just get through this bad period time will take care of you, my friend."

"On a happier note, what are you here for Hon?" Vietnam asked the woman marine.

"Well, at least it's something you guys won't have to worry about. Today is my first day of Chemo Therapy for ovarian cancer."

THE INCIDENT

"Hello, hello, may I have your attention please?" The room grew quiet. "Thank you. My name is Detective Sargent Doerflinger. I am here to investigate the recent incident that occurred in this room. With me is Mrs. Malone, a police stenographer. She will be taking down your answers to my questions."

"I'd like to start with," he glanced at a list of names, "James McLaughlin. Are you here Mr. McLaughlin?"

"Yes, over here."

"Mr. McLaughlin, did you see what happened?"

"No. I was absorbed with some work on my computer screen."

"I see. Thank you. Next is Barbra Miller."

"How can I help you, Sargent Doerflinger?"

"Did you see what happened?"

"No. I had just stepped out to the powder room."

"So you were not in the room when the incident occurred?"

"Yes, that's right."

"In that case, I will have no further questions for you, Ms. Miller. You may go."

"Thank you."

Ms. Miller walked out of the room.

Referring to his list again, Sargent Doerflinger asks, "Is John O'Brien here?"

"Over here."

"Mr. O'Brien, did you see what happened?"

"No, sir. I was eating my lunch at my desk and sort of daydreaming when the incident occurred."

"Thank you. Thomas Cassidy, are you here?"

"Yo."

"Mr. Cassidy, did you see what happened?"

"Nah. I was trying to fix the copy machine when it happened."

"Mary Alice Gregor?" She raised her hand.

"Ms. Gregor, you were a friend of the victim's weren't you?"

"Yes."

"Did you see what happened?"

"No. I was having a personal conversation with Flo at her desk."

Glancing at his list Sargent Doerflinger asks, "Would that be with Florence Kissane?"

"Yeah, with Flo."

"Ms. Kissane, can you confirm Ms. Gregor's statement?"

"Yes. We were both in this deep conversation so neither of us saw the incident."

"Alright, thank you. How about Harry Eginton, is he here?"

"Yes sir"

"Mr. Eginton what is your position with this company?"

"I guess my title would be The Office Boy."

"Thank you. Now Mr. Eginton did you see what happened?"

"No, sir. I was stacking things in the supply cabinet. That one way over there in the corner."

"O.K.. My next question is for Joseph DeLorio. Where are you Mr. DeLorio?"

"Over here, Sargent. You can call me Joe."

"O.K., thank you, Joe. Did you see what happened?"

"No. I was under my desk when the incident occurred. I was having some problem with my computer and I was trying to rearrange the cable connection at the time of the incident."

"I see. Thank you Mr. Delorio."

"You can call me Joe."

"Yes. Finally, I'd like to talk to Arthur Drake."

Looking toward a tall man at the back of the room Sargent Doerflinger asks, "I guess that must be you, sir?"

"Yes, I'm Arthur Drake."

"Mr. Drake, did you see what happened?"

"No. I was in my office, talking on the telephone, and looking out the window when the incident occurred."

"Alright. Thank you, everyone. That is all the questions I have for you. This investigation is closed."

THE MURDER OF MX-133

Mr. Dillingworth murdered his robot, MX-133. He drowned it in the bathtub. Mr. Dillingworth son, Robert, should have been able to predict the murder. After all, he was the director of the Robotics Laboratory at the Massachusetts Institute of Technology. When Robert became aware of his father's deteriorating mental condition, he thought MX-133 was ready for a field trial as caretaker for a human. MIT's Board of Directors was concerned about their liability if anything went wrong with the field trial. However, Robert convinced them that MX-133 was safe and ready and that this field trial would save many months in getting MX-133 ready for commercial production. The prospect of getting MX-133 on the market before anyone else, and gaining domination in the Robotic Home Helper market, was too tempting for the Board to pass up, so they gave him permission to take MX-133 home for a three months test.

The MX-133, now affectionately called Max, was programmed to handle the elder Mr. Dillkingworth's medication schedule, to prepare his favorite meals, do the laundry and general housework. Knowing of his father's curmudgeonly nature, Robert took great care in programming Max's human-interaction programs. To the casual observer, Max would appear to be the ultimate butler, housekeeper, handyman, and companion for the eighty-five-year-old Mr. Dillingworth. The day Robert brought Max home he sensed some tension between his father and the robot, but he attributed it to the newness and novelty of having a robot in the house. He was confident that with time, and Max's human-like programs, things would sort themselves out. They did not. For Mr. Dillingworth it was hate at first sight, but he hid his emotions because he was aware of the importance of the Field Trial to Robert's career.

During the first month of the trial, there seemed to be an uneasy truce between Max and Mr. Dillingworth. Signs of friction began to surface during the second month. It started with the medications. The old man resented being told that it's time for your pills. repeatedly until the pills were swallowed. At first, he tried to fool Max by putting the pills in his mouth but not swallowing them. Max soon caught on and demanded that Mr. Dillingworth open his mouth for a visual inspection.

Then came the arguments over food. Not only was Max a poor cook but he refused to cook with salt. He said he was not programmed for its use. The old man demonstrated four or five times how he wanted his clothes folded. The variety was too much for Max, so he ended up just rolling everything up and stuffing it into a draw.

The final break came when Max turned off the television at 8:00 p.m. and insisted it was bedtime for the old man.

Mr. Dillingworth's dislike for Max grew from hatred to thoughts of murder. It took him a while to come up with the idea of drowning the robot. He did several dry runs to get Max to climb into the bathtub. Max complained that it was Mr. Dillingworth who was supposed to get into the tub, not him. Arguments ensued, but in the end, the human won out, and Max obeyed; all the time insisting that what Mr. Dillingworth wanted was "not logical." On the afternoon of the murder, Mr. Dillingworth ordered Max to get into the tub. When the old man turned on the water, Max panicked and tried to climb out of the rising water. It was as if he knew what was going to happen to him. To thwart the robot's attempts Mr. Dillingworth got into the tub and sat on Max's chest until the water completely covered the robot. MX-133 twisted and turned. His arms and legs began to twitch, and there were several small blue electric flashes. At that point, Mr. Dillingworth got out of the tub and stood looking down at the robot until the twitching stopped and there were no more electrical flashes. He left the body in the tub for two days Television and other Media all over the world picked up the story of the murder. It was publicized as earth-shattering and precedent-setting in that it would determine the legal status of robots worldwide and for generations to come.

In the ensuing trial, the lawyers for MIT claimed that due to Max's many human-like characteristics, the crime was premeditated murder. They argued that if the death penalty was not imposed on the old man, then he should, at least, be sentenced to life imprisonment without the possibility of parole.

The defense lawyer argued two points on behalf of his client. They were that:

(1) the old man suffered from dementia and, (2) that, despite the prosecutor's claim of Max's human-like characteristics, no actual human life was taken.

The judge's instructions to the jury were that they had first to decide whether Max should be considered as a human and, depending on that decision, the jury then had to give its recommendation for the form of punishment, if any.   The jury deliberated for three days and then sent word to the judge that they were ready to announce their verdict.

Spectators and a hundred or more media personnel packed the courtroom when the jury filed in. The judge called for silence and then addressed the foreman of the jury, "Ladies and gentlemen of the jury, have you reached a verdict?"   When the foreman stood up, the onlookers and media people fell silent and held their collective breaths. The foreman turned to face the judge and responded: "Yes your honor we have."   'And what is your verdict?' the judge asked.

"We find the defendant..."

911

The radio lit up, "Auto accident at Vermont Avenue and Wilshire Boulevard," the Dispatcher's voice came through the speaker.

"Unit six responding," the EMT said into the microphone.

The location of the accident was quickly typed into the ambulance's control panel followed by the letters A1. The driver-less ambulance, reacting to the A1 code, turned on its flashing lights and siren, did a U-turn and headed for the site of the accident.

Unit six was the first to arrive at the scene. What they saw was a compact car with a crushed-in roof. The roof was entirely flattened. There was steam coming out of the engine compartment and gasoline dripping from the rear of the small car.

"Looks like it rolled over a couple of times."

"I agree. Lucky for us it landed on its wheels. We should be able to get into it."

"Let's take a look inside first."

"Uh-oh, there's a young girl in there."

"Jaws of life for sure."

"I'll get em." He ran back to the ambulance to get the giant cutting tool.

"Okay, I'll cut, but you need to stand between me and that gasoline to block the sparks. One spark from the jaws and we will all have had it."

It took eight minutes to cut the roof off the car. Together the EMT's lifted the unconscious girl out of the car and placed her on the stretcher. They began to examine her.

"I've got a compound fracture of the right femur here. Tourniquet going on now, just in case the artery breaks." he said.

"Vital signs are all weak but there is still a heartbeat," the other said. "She's gasping for air. Probably a collapsed lung. Oxygen mask and air on." He reported.

"Okay, that's all we can do to stabilize her for now. Let's head to the hospital."

They loaded the stretcher into the ambulance and typed in the code for St. Vincent's hospital followed by the A1 code. With lights flashing and sirens, blaring the driver-less ambulance sped off to the hospital. En route, one of the technicians typed in the information on the girl's condition. When they got to the emergency entrance of the hospital, there was an ER nurse and two orderlies waiting for them. The girl was quickly transferred to a gurney and rushed to a waiting doctor.

"I'll go to the supply room and replenish what we've used," one EMT said.

"Okay, I'll clean up the inside of the ambulance while you do that," the other EMT offered.

Outside of the Emergency room, the two orderlies stopped for a smoke. "Man, that was close," George said.

"Yeah, I didn't think she was going to make it," Emelio replied. "Damn, but those EMT's are good!"

"You got that right. When they first brought in those EMT robots I didn't think they would work out, but those two sure proved me wrong."

THE PEACE CONFERENCE

The goal of the Peace Conference was to implement a system of Government whereby the State Machinery is virtually nil, and the real power resides in the hands of the people. M. G. (1)* Opened the discussion, stress only one condition, namely, let our pledge of truth and nonviolence as the only means for the attainment of peace be faithfully kept. And, that this condition does not give license to all and sundry to carry on t

J. D. (2)* Stands to make a point. "I must emphasize that our true policy is peace and the freest trade which our necessities will permit. It is also our interest, and that of all those to whom we would sell and from whom we would buy, that there should be the fewest practicable restrictions upon the interchange of commodities."

K.M. (3)* interjects, "Yes, yes that, of course, is true but my constituents demand, above all else, a reduction in government spending through a restriction of the bureaucracy and the transference of the major tax burden onto the largest landowners and the merchant class."

M.G. (1)* "It will take leadership to accomplish this. Wherever there are local leaders their orders should be obeyed by the people. Where there are no leaders, and only a handful of men have faith in our cause, they must do what they can, if they have enough self-confidence. They have a right, no it is their duty to do so. History is full of instances of men who rose to leadership, by sheer force of self-confidence, bravery, and tenacity. We too, if we sincerely aspire to peace and are impatient to attain it, should have similar self-confidence. Our ranks will swell and our hearts strengthen, as the number of our arrests by the Government increases."

J.D. (2)* "It must follow, therefore, that a mutual interest would invite good will and kind offices. If, however, passion or the lust of domination should cloud the judgment or inflame the ambition of the Government, we must prepare to meet the emergency and to maintain, by the final arbitration of the sword, the position which we have assumed. It will remain for us, with firm resolve, to appeal to arms and invoke the blessings of Providence on our just cause."

K.M. finalizes the discussion with these solemn words, "You understand, gentlemen, that what we are proposing is nothing less than revolution."

At this point in the discussion, a key can be heard turning in the lock of the wire mesh door leading into the dormitory of the psychiatric unit. The night attendant, nurse Williams, enters and says, "Alright gentlemen it's time for lights out. You can continue this discussion tomorrow. Mr. Ambrose (aka President Jefferson Davis) will you please go to your bed. Mr. Abramovitz (aka Karl Marx) you to yours and Mr. Jalali, (aka Mahatma Gandhi) will you please go to your bed." Mr. Jalali moves quietly to his bed; not at all disturbed by the thought that both his roommates think he is insane.

1) Extracted and edited from Mahatma Gandhi's speech on the eve of the Dandi March, March 11, 1930.

2) Extracted and edited from the Inaugural Address of President Jefferson Davis, Montgomery, Alabama, February 18, 1861

3) Extracted and edited from a speech to The Communist League by Karl Marx, 1850.

WHO WILL CALL OUT

THE ARMY

Articles of Impeachment were drawn up by the House of Representatives. The President was charged with collusion with a foreign power and obstruction of justice. The Senate tried the President and found him guilty of both charges and declared that he was impeached.

The President tweeted that the trial was based on false facts and the trial was rigged. He refused to accept the impeachment verdict. He barricaded himself in the second-floor residence of the White House and refused to leave.

As soon as the Articles of Impeachment were drawn up, right-wing militia groups, a variety of Posse Comitatus groups, the KKK and Neo-Nazi organizations began to descend on the District of Columbia. Most were heavily armed. By the time the President had barricaded himself in the White House, it was surrounded by several thousand-armed supporters who called themselves the Army of Liberation (AL). Cliven Bundy was elected its Supreme Commander. He established his command post in the Trump International Hotel just up the street from the White House. Officers of the AL were housed and fed in the hotel. Tea Party groups, Christian Evangelicals and Right to Life organizations held demonstrations in every major city in the U.S. in support of the president.

The Senate, following its impeachment verdict, tried to appoint a new president as specified in the Constitution. Vice President Pence resigned in support of the President. Speaker Ryan, next in line, refused the appointment, saying it was not the way he had planned it to come about. He resigned as Speaker of the House and moved back to Appleton, Wisconsin.

Turning inward and, again, following the Constitution, the Senate appointed the President pro tempore of the Senate, Orin Hatch, to be the President. Senator Hatch refused the nomination on the grounds of age and poor health.

While these appointments were being offered, the Senate ordered the Capital Police Force to evict the President from the White House. Facing the armed mob surrounding the White House the Chief of the Capitol Police refused to try to breach the cordon on the grounds of 1) being out-gunned and, 2) the order was not within the mandate of the Capitol Police Department.

Meanwhile, back at the Senate, the next appointee to the presidency was Secretary of State Rex Tillerson. He resigned his Cabinet post claiming that he was a corporate CEO and not a general. He was welcomed back to the Exxon Corporation with open arms.

Steven Munchin, the Secretary of the Treasury was next in line for the Presidency. He refused the appointment saying he was a money guy and the presidency would be a bad investment in his future.

Over the next three weeks, the Senate offered Cabinet members the presidency in this order: All refused for various reasons.

Defense Secretary James Mattis, He claimed he was too busy getting the military ready to invade North Korea or maybe Iran.

Attorney General Jeff Sessions. He almost accepted the position but recused himself at the last moment.

Secretary of the Interior, Ryan Zinke He just said no without giving any reasons.

Agriculture Secretary Sonny Perdue. He laughingly claimed he was "To chicken" to be the president,

Commerce Secretary, Wilbur Ross. The U.S. Chamber of Commerce advised against it, so he refused.

Labor Secretary Alex Acosta. He said that since the Teachers Union was hostile to the President that would make the job too difficult.

Health and Human Services Secretary Tom Price, He said the idea of being President made him sick.

Housing and Urban Development Secretary, Ben Carson. Said he would think about it but never got back to the Senate.

Energy Secretary, Rick Perry. He said he wasn't sure what the Presidents job was and, besides, he had his hands full with keeping Texas oil flowing which, he said, was more important than being President.

Education Secretary Betsy DeVos. She asked what the salary was and said it was beneath her to work for such low wages.

The standoff at the White House continued despite Twitter canceling the President's Twitter account. Mark Zuckerberg quickly replaced it with a premium FaceBook account.

In Desperation, the Senate continued its efforts to appoint a president.

Next up was: Veteran Affairs Secretary, David Shulkin who claimed that some of the President's supporters were veterans, perhaps suffering from PTSD, and he could only act in their best interests.

The Senate's last hope, and final member of the Cabinet, was Homeland Security Secretary John Kelly. He said he would not accept the presidency, but he would order FEMA to raise the siege of the White House. FEMA never arrived.

After two months of crisis, the Senate was still faced with the question of who would call out the Army to regain control of the White House.

THE BESTEST COWBOY THAT EVER WUZ

I shore hope no one was lookin' the day I tried to ride that danged bicycle.

Ya see, a cowboy ain't got much he can be proud of or that he can brag about. And I guess it was them three shots of Old Redeye that got me to braggin' in the bunkhouse one night.

I jumped up on the table and shouted, "I'm the bestest cowboy that ever was, and I can ride anything that moves."

"You're drunk," Shorty said. "And git down offen that table 'fore you hurt yourself."

"Well, I may have had a few snorts," I said. "But ain't I the one that rode El Diablo at the Tombstone rodeo? And you all know it was me that was crowned BC [Best

Cowboy] at the El Paso Roundup the year before that. I'm tellin' all you saddle tramps in this here bunkhouse that I can ride anything that moves."

Some of them fellers allowed as how I was maybe a pretty good cowboy at that. So with these acknowledgments of my superior cowboyness, and them three shots of Old Redeye, I was feelin' pretty good. I was about to climb down offen the table when Waco said, "If you're so danged good, how come you ain't rode that bicycle that's leaning up against the barn?"

"What?" sez I. "A bicycle? Why hell, everyone knows a bicycle don't count fer nothin'. No self-respecting cowboy would be caught dead ridin' a bicycle," I said, with a superior look around the bunkhouse. But I could see that some of the fellers was looking doubtful.

I heard someone whisper, "Talks big don't he?"

I hitched up my britches, got down offen the table, and headed for my bunk. "Bicycle," I snorted, and called it a night.

Dear friends, I got to admit, that, after that night, my ego was about as low as a rattlesnake's belly in a road rut. Every time I went past the barn, there that thing was, just daring me to try and ride it. Finally, I couldn't stand it no longer. So one evening just about supper time, when all the other hands were at the dinner table, I decided to show that bicycle who was top hand around this outfit.

I took aholt of that contraption and walked it around to the back side of the barn. Oh, he creaked and squeaked a bit, sort of like any unbroken horse will do, but I've handled enough horses to know not to be intimidated by that kind of stuff. When we got around behind the barn, I stopped for a few minutes to look him over and give him a chance to calm down before I mounted up.True, he only had two legs instead of four, but I reckoned he would be stable enough, so I mounted up. Kabam! . . . No sooner had I hit the saddle when he threw me to the ground. . . . Three times in a row!

Sure, my pride was hurt a bit, but I ain't nothin' if I ain't stubborn, and by the fourth time I mounted him I was beginning to get the feel of him. I figured out that if I pushed the pedals just a bit, it was easier to stay upright. We even began to move ahead a little.

Well, now, this is more like it, I thought. I'll bet . . . . Uh oh, uh oh, he's startin' to trot down this here hill. Pulling back on the handle bars didn't do no good in getting him to slow down. In fact, he was going at a full-out gallop.

Down the hill we went, right through Ms. Bailey's vegetable patch with tomatoes and string beans flying every which a-way. We sideswiped the chicken coop in a cloud of feathers, chickens squawkin' and runnin' in every direction. I do believe one of them died of a heart attack. Straight ahead was the water trough. Well, at least that will stop this beast, I thought. And then I remembered that the water trough was right next to the pig pen!

Well folks, the water trough stopped the bicycle all right, but it gave that danged contraption one last chance to throw me, right over the fence, and into six inches of pig poo.

I gathered myself up and went around to inspect the bicycle. His front wheel was all bent out of shape, and he was hissing air out of his front tire. I could see right off it was a fatal injury, so I did what every good cowboy knows to do when his mount has gone lame. I took out my six-shooter and put him out of his misery.

THE VIOLIN

Time to start another one. Let me see...this will be number...um...279. My how time goes by. The family has been fortunate and we seem to be in some demand. I can only hope that number 279 will live up to our reputation.

He entered the drying room where the treated woods were cured after the harsh chemical soakings. Maple to start with for the back and ribs. Maple again for the neck but not just yet. With a keen eye, years of experience, and a certain sense of excitement that always overcame him with the start of a new endeavor, he sifted through the stacks of treated maple wood. It took him an hour to find a particularly handsome piece. Yes, he thought, this looks very promising. Very promising indeed. How could he explain to anyone the sense of "rightness" that overcame him when he looked at, weighed, and rubbed his hand over a piece of wood? No explanation was possible. He just "knew" this was the correct wood for this new one.

He carried the piece of maple into his workroom and stood by the window to examine it again in the daylight. For thirty minutes, he looked at it from every angle as he appraised the grain and the flatness. He looked carefully for minute cracks and burrs in the grain. There were none. "Yes, very promising indeed," he murmured.

Satisfied that he had found the correct foundation piece for this new item, he ceased work and spent the rest of the day going over the next steps in his mind. As he mentally reviewed the work, he found several points at which he felt he could make some improvements. He determined to put them into practice.

The week that followed consisted of tracing the bottom shape on the piece of maple, cutting it out and sanding, sanding and more sanding. He found one section of the wood that was thicker than he wanted so that needed sanding again. During the course of that week, a premonition took possession of his mind. There is something special about this project he thought with rising excitement. Again, it was beyond explanation, but he knew that "something special" was happening.

Because of this "something special" feeling, he decided to make a fresh pot of glue just for 279. Mixing and boiling the glue took four days. He did it in the family's traditional way and worked slowly to get the consistency just right. In the end, he was satisfied and set the glue pot aside so that no one else in the workroom would use it.

Crafting the ribs was next. He cut them out of the same piece of maple he'd used for the bottom. It was tedious work since there were so many ribs and no two were exactly alike. Each rib was cut, sanded and fitted into its exact place on the bottom piece. It took him eight days to make them and glue them in place but in the end, he was satisfied. Definitely something special happening here. He did not mention it to the rest of the family.

The next several steps took him back to the wood drying room; this time for Willow wood. Willow wood is very delicate and because of the "special nature" of this instrument he spent three days just looking for the right pieces of it— eventually, he found them. They were as graceful as a swan's neck but tight grained and light as feathers. After more shaping and sanding, sanding, and sanding he glued them to the ribs.

The top was, of course, the crucial piece. Again, his instinct, his heart, told him that this project called for, and could sustain, something special. Spruce was the wood for the top but here he tried something daring. Several pieces of spruce wood in the drying room were from Croatia but the family had never used it on any of its products. Nevertheless, he decided to use it for 279. Once he found the piece he wanted he spent two days just feeling it, knocking on it to listen for its resonance, and convincing himself that this was the right thing to do. And it was. As he applied the newly mixed varnish (made of gum Arabic, honey and egg whites) the entire piece seemed to meld itself into a single wooden structure. Now he was sure it was special.

The final steps of adding the neck, the tuning pegs, and the bridge took another week. At last, it was ready. He added strings, tuned it, picked up a bow and played a few scales.

Yes, this one is special! Extraordinarily so. It might even prove to be the best one so far he thought as he applied his label to the inside of the body and read:

Antonio Stradivari, Cremona, Italy 1723.

THE SECOND DATE

UKULELE BLUES

Knock, knock.

"Coming, I'm coming. Just a minute." She took a last look around her apartment and then went to the door.

"Hi." He said

"Hi," She smiled. "Come on in."

He entered and looked around, "Nice place," he said.

"Thank you," she replied modestly. "It's not much but I call it home, and it works for me. Is that your ukulele?" She asked pointing to the small instrument case he was carrying.

"Yep, that's it, just like I promised on our first date."

"Well, I'm impressed. I've never known anyone who could play the ukulele. Would you like some wine? I've got red and white."

"It's a bit early to go for dinner but a glass of red would be nice. Thanks."

She went to the kitchen for the wine. He strolled around the room looking at her photographs, her books and her CD collection. Finally, he took a seat on the sofa and waited for her return.

She came back with a glass of red wine for him and white for herself. She set them on the coffee table and then sat at the opposite end of the sofa facing him. "So, let's hear this ukulele. This should be fun."

He started to open the instrument case and said, "I'm not very good. I've only been playing for a few months, but I love it." He removed the Mala Uke from its case and then attached a small black device to the upper end near the tuning keys. "Gotta tune it up first," he said as he began plucking on the strings one at a time.

"What is that little black thing?" she asked.

"Oh, that's an electronic tuner," he said, still plucking on the strings. "See how the little light turns from red to green as I turn the keys. When they are all in the green, then I know it's tuned up. See now they're all green so we're ready to go. Here's one of my favorite songs." He started to strum the ukulele and began to sing in a quavering voice:

By the light of the silvery moon,

I want to spoon. To my honey

I'll croon loves tune...

The girl smiled politely as he sang, but she looked a bit befuddled. He continued to sing...

Honeymoon keep a shining in June

Your silvery beams will bring loves dreams.

We'll be cuddling soon. By the silvery moon.

"That was...um...nice," she said with a half smile. "I think I heard an actress named Betty Grabel sing that song in some old movie...I think. Do you know any others?"

"Sure, how about this one?" he started playing the ukulele and singing.

Oh we ain't got a barrel of money

Maybe we're ragged and funny

But we'll travel along, singing our song,

Side by side...

He glanced over at the girl and could see that she was looking chagrined. "What's the matter?" he asked. "Don't you like that one?"

"Well, it's sorta' nice, but it sounds terribly old. Do you know any songs by the Electric Funk? They're my favorite band."

"No there are no arrangements for the ukulele by the Electric Funk that I know of. How about this?" He started to play and sing...

Puff the Magic Dragon

Lived by the sea

And frolicked in the autumn mist

in a land called Hon a lee.

Little Jackie Paper loved that

Rascal Puff.....

He stopped playing when he saw that the girl was clearly upset, "But that's a classic song by Peter, Paul and Mary. Don't you like that one either?"

"Peter, Phil and who?" she asked with a puzzled look on her face.

"I Love these old songs," he affirmed. "I just love 'em."

"Do you know any Rap tunes?" she asked.

He shook his head no.

"Any Lead Zeppelin?"

Again, he shook his head negatively. "I know one or two Beetles songs. How about them?" he asked hopefully.

"Oh yes, I heard of them when I was a little girl," she replied. "Look, maybe we don't need the ukulele after all. And besides, it's about time we left for dinner."

"Okay. I know of a nice Chinese restaurant not too far from here." He said

"I don't care for Chinese food," she replied. "I really like French food. Do you know of any French restaurants in town?"

"No, I can't think of a single one. How about Pizza?"

"Ugh, too heavy. There's a nice Indian restaurant just down the street. How about that.?"

"Indian food, like from India? I've never tried it, but sure let's give it a whirl" he said valiantly.

She gathered her purse and a sweater while he finished putting his Ukulele into its case. As they walked out of the apartment He thought Well, so much for that. They'll be no third date here. I wonder how much this Indian restaurant is going to cost me.

She thought Another dead end. I'm going for the top of the menu tonight.

A GOOD MISSION

Novgorod, USSR, November 22, 1944. 4:30 a.m.

Senior Lieutenant Lilya Alexandrovna Belochkin, the pilot, and her crew of four women had been waiting in their Tupolov-2D since 4:00 am. At the mission briefing, the pilots were told to, "Wait for the white flare. That is your signal to proceed with the mission." It was cold, and there was no provision for heat in these new Tupolov's. There were two thermos bottles of tea, but she knew the crew would need them later in the flight. So they were all cold, herself, her co-pilot, the navigator and the two gunners. She and her crew were one of forty-six all-women crews on active duty in the Air Force.

It has been difficult she thought. Ever since she enlisted in 1941 right after Hitler declared war on the USSR, there had been the usual insults and humiliations from the male officers. No separate living quarters for women, no separate toilets. Not even uniforms for women. They had to make do with male uniforms. But we persevered, she thought, and here we sit, waiting to take off on our eleventh mission.

So much for male prejudices!

As she sat thinking, her mind reminisced about her flying career. In 1930 at fifteen she joined a flying club. She started flying for the mail service in 1936. By 1941, she had been flying for commercial services for five years. The Air Force was happy to get her.

The white flare jolted her out of her revere. Time to go.

The Tupulov was a temperamental machine. On landings, one had to watch the angle of decent very carefully and hold it within three or four degrees. Taking off with three thousand pounds of bombs, as she was doing now, required a long run at full power to get it up to flying speed. Crosswinds were no help.

Once they were airborne, and information with the other eighty-seven planes, it was critical to hold her position in the formation since each plane was responsible for protecting the rear of the plane ahead.

She reviewed her course, flying speed and the weather with her navigator. One hour and twenty-two minutes to the target area in Lithuania. , The Pilots were told at the briefing that the area was a marshaling point for German forces getting ready to retreat into Germany. They were also told that the weather over Lithuania was deteriorating.

Twenty minutes out from the target area, the weather had gotten dangerous. The entire squadron would have to descend to 850 meters (2,700 feet) to make their bombing runs. This made them much more vulnerable to the German anti-aircraft guns. Lilya wished they were able to go in at their normal altitude of 1000 meters (3200 feet) where they were much safer.

Two minutes from the target she descended to 850 meters and started her bombing run. Suddenly, the plane in front of her disappeared. It simply vanished, and they were alone in the sky. She continued on course. Thirty seconds later the plane jolted sharply to the right and up about fifty feet. They'd been hit! Fragments of the shell grazed the left engine, entered the cockpit, and hit Lilya in the underside of her right thigh.

Of course, there was pain, but the realization of what had happened, and her fight to regain control of the aircraft overcame the initial pain. I've got to get us out of here was all she could think of. Since the plane was thrown to the right, she instinctively went with it and did a climbing one hundred and eighty-degree turn. Once they reached 2500 feet and headed back towards Russia, she was able to take stock of their situation. The airplane was flyable with one engine, but that was not the problem. The problem was her. She was losing blood from her wound.

"I cannot make it back to Novgorod," Lilya told her navigator. "Find us an alternative landing field nearby." Moments later the navigator told her there was a fighter base at Povno, about twenty minutes away. Lilya changed course and headed for it.

When they got to Povno, they were told that the fighter squadron was in the middle of taking off and that she would have to circle the field until the air was clear...about ten minutes.

By the time they were cleared to land Lilya was dizzy and light headed from loss of blood. Getting the Tupulov on the ground in her condition, and with just one engine, was terrifying and pushed her flying skills to the limit. Once on the ground, her co-pilot was able to taxi the plane off the runway. Lilya shut down the remaining engine and realized that her crew was safe, she had saved the airplane, and she was not going to die. All-in-all a successful mission she thought as she collapsed into unconsciousness.

THE SECRET INGREDIENT

The kettle on the stove hissed as it approached the boiling point. Kate O'Brien ignored the kettle because she was staring, no, glaring into the eyes of her sister-in-law. "You know. I know you know, but your not going to tell me are you?" Kate asked.

Not so fast Katy m'dear her sister-in-law, Bridget O'Brien, thought. You can't come into this family and just take over ya know. Your going to have to work to get this secret out of me.

Bridget smiled at Kate and said, "You know it's a family secret so I can't just give it away."

"But it's Frank's favorite dish," Kate said, "and I promised I'd make it for him on our first anniversary. That's today, and he'll be home in a couple of hours. You've just got to tell me what the secret ingredient is."

"Well, lets see," Bridget said, "You've braised the beef. Right?"

"Yes"

"And you've diced the potatoes and carrots. Right?"

"Of course."

"How about the onions? What kind did you use?"

"Ah, I know about that one," Kate said, "I used pearl onions, not just plain ones."

"You've got that right."

"Yes, I've done all of that right, but I know something is missing. I've tasted your mothers Irish stew and I know there's a secret ingredient in it. You've got to tell me what it is."

Well, we'll just see how clever you are m'girl. I'll give you this hint and see if you get it Bridget thought to herself. "Yes, I know it's Frank's favorite dish and with him out fishing on the bay all day I'm sure he'd appreciate it when he comes home."

'It's hard enough being a fisherman, and the bay is cold this time of year." Kate replied.

Ah, missed it did 'ya, Bridget smiled to herself at the thought. "As for me, I'd just as lief not be out on the bay on a day like this."

"Lief. Now that's a queer word to be using in this day and age," said Kate. "And to be using it in your thoughts about the bay...lief....bay...bay leaf." "BAY LEAF! That's it, bay leaf is the secret ingredient isn't it?" she screamed at Bridget.

Well I practically had to put the words in your mouth. Now lets see if you can get the second part thought Bridget. "Yes," she said, "that's the secret ingredient."

"But how much?" asked Kate, "Too much bay leaf and I'll ruin it. Not enough and it won't have the right taste."

"Kate, I've practically given you the family secret," Bridget replied. "What you're asking now is just too big of a favor."

"How is that too big of a fav ....too big...two big. "TWO BIG BAY LEAVES" shrieked Kate as she dove for the spice rack.

IT COULD HAPPEN

Ronald Frump was a wealthy businessman whom the Republican Party elected President of the United States in 2016. He had business holdings in many countries around the world. These were mainly in the form of hotels, golf courses, and gambling casinos. His children managed his global businesses.

The major policies of his administration were: deregulation, laissez-faire capitalism, economic protectionism and strengthening the military services, To implement these policies he appointed members to his Cabinet who readily followed his wishes. He appointed a recently retired military general as Secretary of Defense. The U.S. military became President Frump's personal police force and the enforcers and protectors of his policies.

As President of the U.S., it was not necessary for Frump to grant favors to the counties in which he had business interests. Those countries made decisions and passed laws that advantaged his family's businesses just to curry favor with the President.

By the end of his first term in office, his wealth had doubled. By the end of his second term he, and his family, were the richest people in the world.

When Frump was elected President in 2016, the Republican Party controlled the Governorship's and Legislatures in twenty-three states. By the middle of his second term in office, that had increased to forty states by gerrymandering and voter suppression techniques.

A two-thirds majority of the Congress passed a constitutional amendment in the middle of his second term. Thirty-eight states approved the amendment within three months and it became the law of the land. The Republican-controlled Supreme Court denied legal challenges to the amendment. The new amendment stated that Ronald Frump was not subject to term limits and is allowed to run for President so long as he lived.

The United States was now an oligarchy.

IT COULD HAPPEN

HE IS ALWAYS
THERE—ALWAYS

His name is Abebe Ambrose, Master Sargent, U.S. Army, (retired). He is distinguished by the military campaign hat he wears. His dress is always immaculate as if he is ready for a general's inspection at any moment. Suit and tie; shoes shined so bright you can see your reflection in them. There's a gold chain around his neck, an American flag and five or six volunteer service pins on the lapels of his suit coat. He carries a cane but doesn't seem to need it much. His back is arrow straight, chest out, and even though he ambles slowly, always appears to be on parade. Abebe is the very model of a first class, African-American, army Drill Sargent.

You'll find him at the VA Medical Center in South Florida. He is not a patient nor an employee, but he is always there —always. 7:00 am to 4:30 pm five days a week. He roams the halls and chats with the staff and patients. They seem to be his family, and he fills the role of a distinguished great uncle.

Ask him what his job is, and he will tell you, "I cure patients by shaking their hand. I cure cancer, loneliness, PTSD, and a number of other critical diseases." Ask him why he does this, and he will tell you, "Because I can. Because they are veterans and my brothers and sisters in arms. Because this country has given me so much. This is my way of paying it back."

And he is always there—always.

FREDDIE-THE-TAILOR

Frederico Schiavonie was born in Naples, Italy in 1868. At the age of fourteen, he was apprenticed to a high fashion, custom tailoring studio. After thirteen years, he earned the title of Master Tailor. In 1895, he married Maria LoTempio and they immigrated to the United States.

As a Master Tailor in the old-world tradition, Freddie had no trouble finding employment in the New York showroom of the Hart, Schaffner and Marx company. He stayed with HS&M until 1908 when he left to open his own studio in the Park Slope neighbourhood of Brooklyn. His specialty was high fashion, custom-made suits for men. When local department stores were selling suits for $35 Freddie was making suits for $200.

By 1910 he had caught the attention of several members of the Black Hand Society, the precursor to the

Mafia. The quality of his materials, the artisanship of his work, and his absolute discretion about the lives of his clients. led to a steady stream of cash heavy gangsters.

The earliest recorded New York gang war was between the Morello and Camorra families. Their rivalry led to the murder of a Morello family member in 1915. His funeral became a matter of "Family Honour" when it was deemed necessary to show the Camorra's that the Morello family would not be intimidated by the murder. With only a few days to prepare for the funeral, the corpse had to be made to look prosperous and important. Freddie was asked if he could accomplish this in the short time allowed. He answered, "Yes but under the unusual circumstances and the time pressure, it would be an expensive proposition." To this, they told him that money was no object.

Freddie put together a costume that consisted of a shirt and tie bib, a suit coat with no back and trousers that went just to the knees since only the upper portion of the casket was open. Everyone agreed that the corps looked elegant.

In 1916 the Morello family retaliated by assassinating a leading member of the Camorra Family. Once again Freddie was called upon to dress the body.

These two funerals were the beginning of Freddie's long reign as the tailor to the mobs. With the clear knowledge that Freddie's services might be needed by anyone, at any time, it was understood that he was a neutral party with no family connection.

The infamous Castellammarese War of 1927 and the Banana (Bonanno) War of 1964-68 were particularly fruitful times for Freddie.

A list of Freddie's most prominent clients paints a colorful picture of the New York Mafia families from 1915 to 1969. After the Camorra and Morello murders there came Giuseppe "Joe the Boss" Messina who was assassinated in a restaurant in Coney Island on April 3, 1931. His murder was followed shortly by that of Salvatore Maranzano on September 10, 1931.

In the years that followed, Freddie attended to various and sundry, small and medium level Mafioso. The murders of big time Mafioso, names that are familiar to us today, started with the assassination of the dreaded hitman, Albert Anastasia, when he was murdered in a barber chair in the Park Sheraton Hotel in 1957. When Vito Genovese died of a heart attack at the US Medical Centre for Federal Prisoners in Springfield, Missouri in 1969 Freddie was summoned to perform his final dressing. In between these "celebrity" deaths, Freddie continued to service his "regular" i.e. non-mob clients, from his small studio in Park Slope. Few, if any, of his regular clients, were aware of his attachment and services to the Mafia families.

Freddie died quietly in his home 1953. Out of respect for his attachment and services to the Mafia Families, his funeral was attended by the President of the Borough of Brooklyn, The New York City Police Commissioner, and a variety of Mafia vips.

DUST BOWL DIARY

Sharecropping is the most common application of the sharefarming principle. In practice, sharefarmers work land which they don't own in return for varying portions of the total profit. In many cases where it is practiced in very poor farming communities, it is considered an exploitative model. Sharecropping began after the Civil War and ended between the 1930s and the 1940s.

Wikipedia: Share farming

Adams, Oklahoma, April 20, 1931

My wife, Ellie, says I should keep this diary so that when our girls, Helen and Jill, grow up they will have it to look back on and be able to remember their childhood. We've been sharecropping these twenty five acres for two years now. The owner, Mr. Askew, is a good man, and he has treated us fairly so far.

Last year was a good year. Wheat was at a dollar fifty five a bushel and we came out a bit ahead of our expenses.

I have just finished harvesting the winter-wheat crop. The weather was good, and the rain came at just the right time. We got thirteen bushels per acre, but the price had fallen to a dollar ten cents a bushel. After the reckoning with Mr. Askew, our share was $1,110. Last year our expenses, for the four of us, were eight hundred dollars so we came out three hundred and eleven dollars ahead for the year. If we can cut our expenses this year, and if the price of wheat holds up, we should be all-right.

Jim Jackson says he will sell me a milk cow for fifteen dollars. It would provide milk for the children, and Ellie says she can make and sell some cheese. Guess I'll buy the cow.

Spring wheat crop goes into the ground next month.

July 25, 1931

No rain for eighty six days.

The cow is doing well, and Ellie is happy with her.

Henry, my old mule, died last week. Fortunately, the spring wheat was in the ground. I can wait until harvest time in September before buying a new mule.

August 10, 1931

Still no rain. The next 15 days are critical.

September 1, 1931

The new mule, Adam, is young and doesn't take to the plow very well. Makes for hard work.

September 6, 1931

Got a few sprinkles in late August and last week. Not much hope for this crop.

September 23, 1931

Disaster. We only got seven bushels per acre and the price has gone down to seventy five cents a bushel. After settling with Mr. Askew, I owe him five hundred and eighty seven dollars. He says he will lend me enough money for the seed for the winter-wheat crop. But he is limiting my credit at the grocery store to three hundred dollars.

Winter-wheat crop goes in the ground next week, if the rains come back, and the price of wheat goes back up, I should make enough to pay off all these debts; but, there won't be much left over.

Ellie is pregnant.

March 5, 1932

It's official, we are in a drought. No rain in six months.

May 10, 1932

Nothing came out of the ground. No crop at all. I owe Mr. Askew twelve hundred dollars. No credit at the grocery store. Mr. Askew says that since nobody is farming anyhow, we can stay in the cabin for now.

Ellie's garden will have to feed us. There's no hay for the cow, so she will dry up soon. Since I can't get any money for seed, and it looks like the drought will continue, I will try to sell the mule.

The soil is so dry, the wind is starting to carry the topsoil away.

August 25, 1932

It's a boy! Donald. Seven pounds, thirteen ounces. The ten dollars I got for the mule just covered the midwife expenses.

September 24, 1932

I butchered the cow. It was very upsetting to the girls.

December 22, 1932

This is a hard winter. I made up a batch of flour paste and papered the inside of the cabin with newspaper. That helped some, but not much. The school has closed for the winter. Don't know whether or not it will open again. With the girls at home and the new baby, Ellie has her hands full. I got some carpentry work for a couple of weeks, but no more in sight.

March 28, 1933

Roosevelt was elected President. He says that "the only thing we have to fear is fear itself." If he were in my place, he would know what real fear is like.

May 12, 1933

Wheat is down to thirty cents a bushel. Don't make no difference though, because nobody is planting anyway.

June, 1933

I have to give President Roosevelt credit. He got a law passed that allows the Department of Agriculture to distribute food to folks in need. Two times a month we can get three pounds of cheese, two pounds of lard or cooking oil, five pounds of rice or wheat, and three pounds of powdered milk. Not much, but we can survive on it.

August, 1933

The WPA is starting a work program on the county road. I've been hired for two months at fifty-two dollars and fifty cents a month. It will help to have real cash money.

November, 13 1933

This past year has been so bad, I couldn't bring myself to write much about it but something historic happened two days ago, and I feel I must put something down in this diary. Officially, they are calling it a dust storm. Since we have had no rain since October 1931, the ground here has just dried up and turned to powder. Two days ago, November 11, 1933, the wind started to blow with a fierceness beyond anything anyone here has ever seen. In the middle of the afternoon the sky turned black, and you could hardly see your hand in front of your face. The wind-blown sand practically scrubbed the skin off your body. The sand penetrated everything. It came through the cracks around the windows and doors and got into our food. Today we even found sand in the clothes that were folded up in the dresser. Someone said they found sand inside the vault of the bank when they opened it this morning.

January 11, 1934

Oklahoma and Texas are now called the Dust Bowl of America. We are still in a severe drought, and the wind and dust are devastating the land and the people hereabouts. We are living in the land of poverty. Families are starting to leave and moving to California in hope of finding work.

An unusual source of food has come our way recently. The drought has forced millions of rabbits to come down from the foothills in search of food and water. They have become such a pestilence that some weekends we have a rabbit roundup. At first we killed them with shotguns, but that became too expensive, so now we herd them into a wire corral and send young boys in with clubs to kill them. Last week I brought home fifteen of them. Ellie stewed and fried some, and I made jerky out of the rest. Not much, but it's food.

May 10, 1934

Two days of the worst dust storms so far. We were trapped in the house. Several people got caught outside and died. I am at my wits' end as to how to feed my family and keep us alive. I haven't been to church in years, but now we all go on Sunday. Has God forsaken us?

April 18, 1935

They're calling it Black Sunday. Starting on April 14,1935, we had three days of a dust storm of historic proportions. I'm told it swept through the entire Oklahoma Panhandle and as far south as Amarillo, Texas.

It covered thousand of square miles. When we looked out the window two days later, everything was covered with sand: the fences, the wagon, and half way up the side of the house. There was nothing to see for miles around but an ocean of sand.

April 25, 1935

Donald is having trouble breathing. It's called Dust Bowl Pneumonia. Very worried for him.

April 30, 1935

Donald is dead.

Ellie and I and the girls are leaving this awful place. We will follow the other Oakies to California and hope for the best.

ONE AND ONE MAKES TWO

Joe Mazarek was raised in an orphanage in Pittsburgh, Pennsylvania. Despite his best efforts he never located his parents. Joe managed to get his GED high school certificate and stay out of jail. In 1998 Joe, now 21, was flipping burgers at minimum wage and going nowhere. Anything would be better than this he thought, so he joined the Army and found a home.

Ten years later he had risen to the rank of Sargent and was the squad leader of an infantry platoon. In 2008 he stepped on a land mine in Afghanistan and lost his right leg just below the hip.

Helen Wilson was a fun loving high school cheerleader from Dayton, Ohio. She earned her AA degree from a local community college and, despite her father's recent death, went on to get a degree in Psychology from the

University of Cincinnati. By the time Helen reached 24 her mother had begun to show signs of dementia.

Out of desperation, and faced with the rising financial burden of her mothers care, Helen joined the U.S. Air Force in 2004 when she learned that, as Helen's dependent, her mother's care would be taken over by the Air Force. Helen was given the rank of Second Lieutenant and learned to fly helicopters. Her mother passed away two years later.

In 2008, while on a rescue mission in Iraq, her helicopter was hit by a rocket propelled grenade and Helen's left leg was blown off just below the knee.

Joe and Helen met at the rehabilitation center at the Bethesda National Medical Center in Baltimore.

Their friendship blossomed into a brother and sister-like relationship

One day, after a particularly hard session of trying to walk with the aid of parallel bars, Helen called Joe over and said "Let's try something. Come stand on my left side and let me put my arm around your shoulder. Hold me around the waist. Now I'm going to lean on you and step forward with my right leg, then you lean on me and step forward with your left leg."

It actually worked.

By leaning and alternately stepping they managed to move around the room. They both laughed and thought this was great fun. With practice they were soon making their way around the hospital and even into the cafeteria to the great delight of the hospital staff.

When asked why this co-dependency worked so well for them they would reply "Because one and one makes two" It wasn't long before they were being referred to as "That One-and-One couple."

Eventually Helen came down with pneumonia and died after a two week struggle. She was buried in the military cemetery in Arlington Virginia.

Two days after Helen's funeral Joe was found hanging in a linen room. The note pinned to his chest asked that he be buried next to Helen because "One and one makes two."

THANK YOU, TEDDY ROOSEVELT

Teddy Roosevelt formed the Progressive Parry in 1912. He did this in response to a split in the Republican Party between him and William Howard Taft. In founding the Progressive Party Roosevelt aligned himself with the Progressive Movement that had been growing in the country since 1890.

Roosevelt and the Progressive Party gave enormous prestige to the standing of the Progressive Movement and allowed many progressive policies to become the law of the land. This resulted in a number of educational reforms and, notoriously, Prohibition In the realm of housing and urban design New York progressives were able to build upon the Tenement House Act of 1901. This was a landmark victory against the "old tenement houses" which were blamed for high rates of tuberculosis and other infectious diseases caused by crowding, lack of sanitation facilities, and ventilation in the older buildings. Under the Progressive interpretation of the new housing act, the "new tenements" were required to have one toilet facility per apartment and one or more interior light courts to bring light and air to the interior rooms of the buildings. By the 1930's thousands of "new tenement" buildings had been erected in New York City. The majority of these were five or six-story walk-up apartment buildings; all with interior courtyards.

Interior courtyards engendered a number of social and behavioral changes in the residents and gave rise to a neighborhood culture which was unique for the period from 1929 to the end of WWII.

Interior courtyards opened up a new world to street vendors and peddlers. By taking their wares and services into the courtyards vendors no longer had to wait for shoppers to come down to the street level. Now the vendors could bring their goods right up to the doorstep of the residents. This ability, plus the change from horse-drawn wagons to motorized trucks, created a new kind of "stay at home consumerism." The milkman could now enter through the courtyard and deliver milk to every apartment in the building. Bakery companies followed suit. Dugan's bakery was one of the leaders in this trend. It did well for many years with the slogan "Thomas' promises but Dugans delivers" The Dugan company distributed twelve inch by twelve-inch cardboard cards with a big letter D on them to every household in a neighborhood. All the shopper had to do was place the card in a window and the Dugan man would bring the basket of today's offerings to the apartment door. The same was true for the Iceman. In this case, the card had a number on each of its edges, 15, 25,35,50 (cents). The consumer placed this card in his/her window with the appropriate edge up and the iceman would deliver ice right into their ice box. This was a new, more convenient kind of consumerism.

Street musicians soon started using the courtyards for fifteen to twenty-minute concerts, mostly on the accordion or violin. Householders, who were so inclined, would wrap a few coins in a piece of newspaper and throw them down into the courtyard as payment. The sound of music bouncing off the walls of the courtyard was reminiscent of music in the New York or Paris subway tunnels.

Knife sharpeners or pot menders would push their grinding wheels into the courtyard and set up temporary shop to do their repairs.

On hot days the shaved-ice man would push his art into the courtyard to the delight of children and adults alike. The man with the Charlotte Rouses' usually came in the late afternoon or just after dinner. By the time the Charlotte Rouse made its way to New York—especially to sweet shops in Brooklyn and the Bronx—the confection had taken a dramatically simplified form. It was made from a thin disk of sponge cake placed in a paper tube and topped with a lofty swirl of whipped cream and crowned with a Maraschino cherry. Variations included sprinkles, chocolate-flavored whipped cream, or a spoonful of jam nestled between the cake and the cream. It was sold from pushcarts, candy stores, and bakeries (primarily, but not exclusively, Jewish ones) mainly to eager school kids seeking the ultimate afternoon snack.) Wikipedia

Eventually, the Good Humor Man with his truck and bells and the man in the vegetable truck made their way into these middle-class neighborhoods.

The courtyards made a safe place for children to play.

The combination of all these activities made it virtually impossible not to interact with your neighbors. Birthday parties, street parties, summer fire hydrant parties, stickball games on the street, neighborhood elementary schools, synagogues, and churches provided the social fabric that led to the concept of "my neighborhood" which became the emotional anchor for many, many lives.

So, thank you, Teddy Roosevelt.

MÉNAGE A TROIS

It started with a baguette.

Ah, but wait, first you must know the background and the setting. The sunshine was glorious, the afternoon air was balmy the atmosphere was sultry. Breakfast had been light so there was room for indulgence. My agenda was clear. There were no pressures to do anything so a casual trip to Whole Foods was completely in order.

Then I saw the baguette.

You must know that "Nothing white" (especially not white bread) has been my mantra for twenty years. But, one glance at that baguette and I felt twenty years of abstinence melting away. After all, my last real baguette had been in Paris almost thirty years before. Resisting those limp, tasteless, eunuch-like, American baguettes had not been a problem. As a voyeur in the bakery section of Whole Foods, I was taken aback by what seemed to be a real baguette. My hand trembled as I reached out to touch its tawny brown skin-like crust. Yes, yes the crust was firm to my loving caress!

There comes a time in every life when caution, rational thinking, and years of tradition should be thrown aside. I knew I had reached that moment. Cholesterol be damned I thought as I abandoned all restraint and took the plunge into gastronomic bliss. I bought the baguette.

Oh no, gentle reader, do not think this was going to be a crude, rough and tumble tryst between just me and the baguette. In for a penny, in for a pound. This would be a true, old-world tryst in the French style. The baguette was just the beginning, the foundation so to speak.

Baguette tucked safely under my arm I descended upon the cheese department. Careful now, nothing too fancy...certainly not brie or a goat cheese. A Dutch Gouda would be too smoky and a German Dortmund too bland. Several Italian candidates caught my eye for a moment but in the end, I settled for tradition and reliability...a four-year-old English white cheddar...that was the ticket!

Since this gastronomic orgy was to be in the French style, the final ingredient was a fine butter. Only a brilliant yellow, Irish butter would do.

Needless to say, there would be no nonsense with any mustards or mayonesses. Not even a good Sicilian Olive oil would be allowed into this party.

I could hardly wait to get home with my treasures.

In the end, the baguette, while lacking the delicate inner texture of a real Parisian baguette, held its own. Yes, it was an American baguette and the crust required a firm bite but once through the crust, the inner treasure revealed itself with just a wisp of yeast taste. The full sequence, of course, was: first, a not too thick smear of Irish butter (who but the French would eat cheese with butter) then a generous slab of the cheddar. The baguette made the cheese taste better. The cheese made the baguette taste better and the butter tied both together with the skill of a Swiss diplomat.

Baguette, butter, cheese and voilá my Mènage a trios was complete and I was in food heaven.

Will I ever be able to return to "Nothing white"?

THE VORTEX

Vortex *n* a whirling mass of fluid or air, especially a whirlpool or a whirlwind — a swirling vortex of emotions.

"God Damn horse," Goodman exclaimed "it's costing me a fortune to keep, and it hasn't earned enough to pay for the hay it eats."

"That's typical for the racing business," the stable master commiserated.

Well, I'm going to find a way out of this mess Goodman thought.

The answer came about a week later when he met an alcoholic veterinarian, whose license had been revoked, at a near-by track bar. "Insurance," the Vet said over drinks provided by Goodman. "First get the horse to win some races, which makes him more valuable, and then you buy more life insurance on him. When the insurance is high enough you kill-off the horse, collect the insurance, and get out of the racing business."

"Nice idea," Goodman said, "but I see a couple of problems. First, how do I get this dog of a horse to win some races? And second: how do I kill the horse without the insurance company crying 'Murder' and refusing to pay on the policy?"

"That's where I come in — for a fee," the Vetr replied. "I will supply you with a steroid cocktail, which you will give to the horse, gradually, over the next eight months. That's how he will win some races so you can add to his insurance policy. When you are ready I will give you a final, untraceable, cocktail that will burst his heart and make it look like he died of heart failure."

"Sounds illegal to me," Goodman said.

"It is," the Vet replied.

The following two days were spent in negotiating the vet's fee and detailed explanations on how to gradually administer the steroids to the horse. When Goodman was convinced the scheme was doable he began to put it into motion. The plan was to be carried out over the next ten races. It was agreed that the horse would be allowed to win six of the ten races just to justify the increase in his insurance policy.

What Goodman did not know was that the vet was burning the candle at both ends. From his years of experience at the race track, he had become acquainted with a number of professional gamblers. Once the insurance scheme was hatched he contacted "Benny Bets" Benson a well-known figure in horse racing circles.

"This could be big," Benny Bets told the vet, "even after you get your cut."

A couple of days later Benny and the vet met again. "Okay, here's how it's going go down," Benny said. "I've put together a group of big money horse players — call it a consortium — there are ten of us. We are going to place bets on this horse, even on the losing races, so no one gets suspicious. We will make money on the six races he wins. When you tell us the horse has had about all he can take we will make our big bets. The winnings, less your cut, will be divided evenly amongst the consortium members. One more thing, the owner must not know about the consortium. We don't want him to get greedy and start making his own bets. Got it?"

"Okay, I'm with you on this." The vet promised.

Johnny Fortunato was the horse's jockey. One of the things he shared with the stable manager was a genuine love of horses. At age twenty-three he had spent most of his life around them, Now, as a professional jockey, he considered himself lucky to be doing what he loved best. In the case of this particular horse, Johnny's sympathies lay more with the horse than with its owner. He knew that this horse was never going to be one of the great ones but race after race Johnny felt, he knew, that this horse was doing the best he could. Johnny could feel the courage, fortitude, and spirit this horse was pouring into every race. A bond had formed between the horse and the jockey.

As the insurance scheme unfolded Johnny sensed that something strange was happening though he was unaware of the details. By the time they got through the sixth race with three wins and three losses, Johnny was certain the horse was being doped.

He told the stable master of his suspicions who shrugged and said, "This can be a dirty business kid, keep your nose out of it and just ride the best races you can."

Goodman was satisfied with the way the scheme was playing out. So far the pattern of wins and losses had not raised any suspicions. He had purchased more insurance on the horse.

The consortium was watching the wins and losses carefully. The vet told them that races seven and eight would be wins. Number nine would be a loss so as not to arouse any suspicions. The tenth would be a win and the final race for this horse. He would be dead before the eleventh was scheduled.

Johnny Fortunato was beside himself with concern for the horse's health. It was acting skittish and it was hard for Johnny to keep him under control. Each time they won a race the horse would go from a pre-race high to a post-race low marked by erratic behavior.

The loss of the ninth race seemed to calm the horse down somewhat. His behavior returned to normal much to Johnny's relief.

By the day of the tenth race Goodman, the consortium and Johnny Fortunato were in a swirling vortex of emotions.

Goodman was glad the scheme was coming to an end without being discovered by the Racing Commission.

The consortium placed a medium sized fortune on this race spread out over many bets. One cannot be too sure about the outcome of a horse race and they were apprehensive. So far the consortium considered itself lucky but the stakes on this race were enormous.

Johnny Fortunato knew that some sort of climax had been reached. Before the race, the horse was acting like a wild stallion. Johnny stroked him and talked to him in the tenderest tones...almost to no avail.

The tenth race started out as planned. By the halfway point around the track, Johnny and the horse started to take the lead. At the three-quarter point, they were ahead by half a length. Between the three-quarter point and the finish line, the horse started to stagger. Ten yards from the finish line the horse's front legs collapsed. It fell forward on to its chest throwing Johnny into the path of three following horses. Two of them smashed Johnny's skull with their hooves. He was dead before he realized what was happening.

By the time the ambulance reached Johnny the horse was also dead.

Because there was the death of a jockey and the unusual nature of the horse's collapse, the Racing Commission announced that there would be a thorough investigation of the incident. The post-mortem study of the horse's remains revealed an enormous amount of steroids in the horse's tissue and especially its heart.

The jockey's death was ruled an accident.

The tenth race was declared null and void and no bets were paid.

Goodman was found guilty of malfeasance, race tampering, and animal cruelty. He was sentenced to two years in prison.

The veterinarian was found dead of alcohol poisoning behind a track bar.

The members of the consortium took their losses as part of the racing life and each went their own way.

UNCLE JIM AND THE BEAR

This story that I'm about to tell you is a true story. I know it's a true story because it was told to me by my grandfather and everyone knows that grandfathers never tell a lie. When Granddad's uncle Jim retired from the railroad he built himself a cabin in the woods. It had a nice view of a lake and a front porch where Uncle Jim could sit and watch the sun go down. He said he'd had enough of civilization and now all he wanted was peace and solitude.

I come from a large musical family with a long tradition of musicians and singers and Uncle Jim was no exception to that tradition. So once he'd settled down Uncle Jim began pining for some music in his solitary life so he invented a fine musical instrument. It is a one stringed instrument and is a sort of cousin to a banjo. If you can imagine a stick about three feet long with an empty tin can on one end and a tuning peg on the other. Then imagine a single banjo string running from the tuning peg on one end and through the tin can on the other end of the stick and you'll have an idea of what this instrument looked lie. You play it like a banjo and just pick out tunes on that single string. Uncle Jim called it a Canjo.

Well sir, Uncle Jim started to teach himself to play the Canjo and he started with his favorite song: You Are My Sunshine.

Unfortunately a problem developed when he came to the very last note in that song. For some reason it sounded terrible. Now Uncle Jim knew that the correct not was somewhere on the Canjo but he just couldn't find it. Night after night and week after week he sat out on his front porch and searched and searched for the lost note.

About that time some of Jim's neighbors started talking a bout a ferocious bear that was ravaging the countryside thereabouts. Rumor was that this bear had already killed a sheep and two dogs. Folks also believed that the bear had a den in the woods not far from Uncle Jim's cabin.

Of course, Uncle Jim was worried to hear all this so he began putting a thick wooden bar across his front door every night when he went to bed.

Then one night, just after Jim got into bed, he began to feel the ground around his cabin starting to tremble. And it got worse and worse and seemed to be moving out of the woods right toward the cabin. Sure enough it was the bear and Jim was certain it was coming for him.

Pretty soon the whole cabin was shaking, and the next thing Jim knew the bear was right out there on the front porch. Now you've all seen how a bear can get up on it's hind legs and push against something with his front paws...well that's what the bear started doing...pushing against the cabin door fixin' to break it down. The wooden bar started to bend and creak and with one mighty push the bear broke the bar and pushed that door right down. Lickey split, the bear was in the cabin.

Poor Uncle Jim was sure the end had come. All he could do was cower in a corner with his arms over his head started saying his prays and wait for the bear to come get him.

And he waited, and waited, and waited — but nothing happened. Pretty soon Jim got up enough courage to peak out from under his arms so see what the bear was going to do. And when he looked around the bear was gone! Jim couldn't believe his good luck. Slowly, little by little, he got up from the corner and surveyed the cabin. Everything was in perfect order. Not a thing had been touched. Finally Jim noticed that the only thing missing was the Canjo. Yep, that bear had stolen the Canjo.

The next morning He repaired the front door and spent most of the day just being grateful that he had escaped a horrible death under the teeth and paws of that huge bear.

That evening, as usual, Jim went out and sat on his front porch to watch the sun go down. After a while he began to hear music coming out of the nearby woods.

What he heard was a perfect rendition of You are My Sunshine...including the perfectly played last note. Yes sir, that Bear had found the lost note.

Now, according to my Grandfather, what happened next was that Uncle Jim and the bear became good friends. Jim made a second Canjo, and he and the bear spent the rest of their days sittin' on the front porch playing Canjo duets 'til the end of their days.

MATVEY ALEXIEVICH AGAPOV'S LETTER TO THE CZAR

In 1842 Nicholas, I was the Czar of Russia. He liked to be known as The Father of all the Russia's, and he often referred to his care for his subjects as being "Like a father to his children."

One of the Czar's "children" was a peasant farmer by the name of Matvey Alexievich Agapov who lived fifty kilometers from the city of Novgorod in Central Russia. This was an underdeveloped and isolated section of the country. Matvey lived with his wife, Agnessa, and Masha, his elderly mother. They were the poorest of the poor of the Czar's "children." Their farm consisted of two fields. In one, they grew cabbages, carrots, and potatoes. In the other, they grew hay for their plow horse, Valya, (whose name means strong and vigorous.) Sometimes in the winter, Matvey was able to catch a rabbit in his trap. This was always an occasion for celebration and thanksgiving for a meal with "real meat" With these two small fields, and the indispensable help of Valya, the horse, Matvey was hardly able to eek out a living for himself, his two dependents, and his horse. Theirs was the peasant's life of hardship, deprivation and almost total ignorance of the outside world.

One morning in November Matvey went to the barn to begin his daily chores. When he looked into Valya's stall, he found the horse lying on his side...dead. Matvey reckoned that Valya had died of old age and exhaustion from the heavy work on the farm. Catastrophe! Matvey thought to himself. Without a plow horse, how will I plant my field in the Spring? There will be no food for next winter. Surely, we will die of starvation.

A broken man, Matvey stumbled back to the house and broke the unfortunate news to Agnessa. When the extent of the catastrophe dawned on her, she cried and wailed as if Valya had been a child of her own.

For the next several days Matvey, Agnessa, and Masha moped around the farm in a fog of hopelessness and despair. What to do? What to do?

And then, one day, as if by a miracle, Matvey had a flash of inspiration that he knew must be the answer to his problem. He would write a letter to the Czar! Wasn't the Czar the father of all the Russias? Didn't the Czar say he was like a father to all his "children"? In his desperate hour of need could a father deny help to the poorest of all his children?

Yes, he would write a letter to the Czar and explain that Matvey's neighbor had a horse that he would sell for twenty rubles (an impossible and unthinkable sum to Matvey) and would the Czar please send the twenty rubles to Matvey as quickly as possible and certainly before the time for next Spring's plowing.

Matvey and Agnessa could read and write...with some difficulty. But a pen, paper, ink and an envelope were not to be found on their farm. It took them three days to find a neighbor who had these things and was willing to trade them for several kilos of carrots. Together Matvey and Agness spent two days composing the letter to the Czar and explaining their desperate need for twenty rubles. Finally, the letter was ready. After much hand washing, it was carefully folded and put into the envelope. Not knowing the correct address Matvey just wrote "To the Czar" on the envelope.

The mail system in that isolated part of Russia consisted of a mailman, Fyodor Boryaovich Dernov, who drove a small wagon that served as a traveling post office. He would drop off and pick up mail, sell stamps, etc. His circuit brought him past Matvey's farm about once every two weeks. Fyodor did not know Matvey very well. He had only delivered one letter to him in the last ten years. Theirs was a nodding acquaintance, but Fyodor thought of Matvey as a hard-working peasant who did not beat his wife, supported his mother and did not cause any trouble in the community. What more could you ask of any man?

Fyodor considered himself, as the official Mailman of the district, to be the living representative of the Czar. Didn't he have the cap with the Czar's coat of arms in the form of a brass medallion, pinned to it?

He was surprised one day when Matvey stopped his wagon to buy a five-kopek stamp. His surprise turned to alarm when he saw the envelope addressed "To the Czar." Such impudence! Fyodor thought And how dangerous! Didn't this peasant realize that the police might come and drag him away for pestering the Czar? Still, whatever is in that letter must be important to Matvey or he wouldn't have dared to write it. I'll let him post it and, later, I'll have a look and see what this is all about.

So Fyodor Dernov sold Matvey the stamp, explained that he had to lick it, and showed him where to place it on the envelope. With great ceremony and many handshakes, Matvey turned his letter over to the mailman. He also wished him God Speed, have a safe journey, and good health.

Later that evening Fyodor steamed the envelope open over his tea kettle and read the letter. Now Fyodor Boravich Dernov was a kindly man, and his heart went out to Matvey and his family, and he began to wonder if there was something he could do to help these poor people survive the coming winter. After much deliberation, he decided that he would explain Matvey's situation to the farmers on his mail route and ask them to contribute whatever they could towards the needed twenty rubles.

In six weeks' time, he was able to raise the twenty rubles. He had exhausted all his resources and a lot of his good will among the local farmers. But he had the money!

Fyodor put the twenty rubles into the envelope Matvey had given him, crossed out the words "To the Czar" and wrote "To Matvey Alexievich Agapov" on it.

Two days later the mailman stopped his wagon at Matvey's farm and blew his whistle to indicate that he had a letter to deliver. Convinced that the letter from the Czar had finally arrived Matvey, his wife Agnessa, and his elderly mother, Masha all went out to the mail wagon to see if their wishes had come true. Fyodor asked if he could stay to witness the Czar's answer. "Yes, yes, of course," Matvey answered, as, with trembling hands, he opened the envelope and took out the twenty rubles. The mailman smiled inwardly and felt the glow of self-satisfaction that comes with knowing he had done a good deed.

Matvey counted the money three times, all the while maintaining an excited chatter and smile while at the same time showing the money to Agnessa, Masha, and the mailman.

"God bless Czar Nicholas," Matvey said over and over again. "He is truly the father of his children. See how he has blessed us." These and other praises in exaltation to the Czar poured forth from everyone witnessing the wonder and spectacle of largess from the Czar. Matvey, his wife, and mother embraced each other in several group hugs out of sheer joy. At one point they even drew Fyodor, the mailman into a group hug.

When at last some composure was regained, and Matvey and his family turned to go back to their house the mailman heard Matvey say "Next year I will ask the Czar for a milk cow!"

Fyodor Boravich Dernov, the mailman, and self-appointed representative of the Czar blanched to a pure white, swallowed hard, took a deep breath and then thought to himself A milk cow! Now where am I going to find a milk cow?

THE UGLY GIRL AND THE BEAUTIFUL WOMAN

By the age of five, she knew she was ugly. Up until that time, the word "ugly" had had no meaning for her, but now she knew what it meant, and that it applied to her. She was not sure which of her physical characteristics caused her parents to turn from warm and loving to cold and indifferent. Certainly, they continued to do their parental duty of clothing and feeding her but their indifference seeped through. Eventually, she sensed the same feeling from aunts, uncles, and cousins. That was when she started to think of herself as an "outsider"— not part of the family.

At first, the school had been a refuge for her and, initially, there had been one or two friends. Once the brutality of social cliques and popularity started to take hold, she found herself an outsider and a loner once again. At this age, she was able to look into a mirror and see what others saw. A round face with puffy cheeks, deep-set eyes, a long sloping nose that divided the left and right halves of her face into two incompatible pieces, an overly large mouth that twisted upwards on one side, crooked teeth, and a chin that protruded forward as if to meet her nose on its slide downward. Scraggly, mousey hair that did not respond to brushing and was unable to hide her too-large ears. The rest of her body followed suit and complimented the ugliness of her face and head.

Her teen years were emotionally tormenting. Didn't every young girl didn't want to be pretty, to be popular, go to dances and proms, have first dates and a boyfriend; to fall in love?

Once the school years were over and she faced adulthood, she was able to visualize her future. There would be no lover, no husband, no children, no home and family of her own.

In her early twenty's she began to wonder about sex with a man. What was it like? Was she ever to find out?

Despair, anger and, finally, bitterness set in.

Her only redeeming feature was her mind. It was keen and all-absorbing. Her intelligence grew with the years and it was the vigor of her mind that allowed her to see her life for what it was and to accept the fate that she had been given even if the disappointment and bitterness remained.

Still, she had to make a living and computer coding at the Jet Propulsion Laboratory in Pasadena, California, came naturally to her. JPL became her sanctuary and the anchor in her life.

She had her own cubicle and her own projects. Interaction with co-workers was minimal and cordial enough but she remained a loner. Her computer was her best friend. Then one day it stopped working. It had to be saved! All her files and projects were in its memory banks. Several people in her department tried to bring it back to life with no success.

"Time to call the Techies," they said.

"Okay, I'll send someone over," the Boss Techie promised.

It took three days to find and solve the problem with her computer. He was not ugly, quite normal looking in fact, but pathologically shy. Out of kindness, she asked him to go to lunch on day two. He talked about being a pathologically shy man in today's world. She spoke about being an ugly girl in today's world.

Who can say how love begins? Or when?

Theirs was slow to start.

At first, it was just friendship and someone to eat lunch with. Then, as friends, someone to do things with. A movie, a basketball game, an opera. And so it grew. As it grew they moved deeper and deeper into each other's souls and psyches. She was able to show him his inner strength and boost his self-confidence. He truly came to understand that she would always be there for him. He filled her need for someone to love. And by returning her love she came to see what was so clear to him— her inner elegance

It took a year of courage for them to realize, and then savor, the bond that formed between them. Their shared intelligence allowed them to bask in the wonder of what had come into their lives. The pace at which their love grew was deliberate and honest. Eventually, it developed an existence of its own. As their love and companionship matured her despair, anger and bitterness melted away. In time, she morphed from an ugly girl into a woman of kindness, composure, honesty, confidence, steadfast helpfulness and love—a beautiful woman.

BLUEBELL AND THE SPIDER

"Eeekkkkkkk," Bluebell the Fairy shrieked, flapping her wings frantically she flew backward and hovered about four feet from where she had been sitting.

"What is it? What's the matter?" Gardenia asked.

"There's a big spider right next to where I was sitting. Give me a fly swatter or a newspaper so I can kill it."

"Kill it? Now wait just a minute before you do anything as rash as that. Killing is forever, and you might regret it later. Did the spider bite you?"

"No."

"Did it harm you in any way?"

"No."

"Well then, let's just think about this for a minute," said Gardenia, an older and wiser fairy. "That spider might be a Mommy spider. Would you want to deprive her children of their Mother?"

"No," Bluebell answered contritely.

"Maybe that spider is a great philosopher. Would you want to deprive all the other spiders of its wisdom?"

"Of course not," Bluebell answered sheepishly.

"That spider could even be a great poet or artist."

"I never thought of it that way," Bluebell said. "But spiders are creepy-crawly things. They're not like us at all. And they eat flies."

"Humans are not like us. And they eat chickens, so do you want to kill humans too?"

"Hmm."

"I'll tell you what, let's wait until tomorrow. If you still think you want to kill that spider, then you just go ahead and do it. How would that be?" Gardenia asked.

"Okay, I guess that's reasonable. I'll wait until tomorrow."

Dawn came up as a rosy red sunrise. Bluebell flew back to the tree where she had seen the spider the day before. When she arrived, she was astonished to see a huge web that went from the lowest limb of the tree down to the very stump that Bluebell had been sitting on the day before. The web was spun in intricate geometric and circular patterns. It had diagonal strands that added interest and contrast to the circular forms. This marvelous creation was covered with morning dew. The light from the rising sun refracted through the dew drops covering the beautiful web with all the colors of the rainbow. The spider web looked like a giant, fantastic, colored crystal.

It was the most beautiful thing Bluebell had ever seen.

Gardenia was right, Bluebell thought, this spider is a great artist. I was foolish to even think about killing it just because it is different than I am.

Bluebell sat down, reveling at the spider's beautiful creation; and then, after a while, she flew away.

TONY SCARFANO

Tony Scarfano was in love, but he didn't know it. He didn't know he was in love because he did not know what love was. There had never been love in his life; not from his parents, there had never been a loveable toy, or a pet, or a friend at school, or a teacher, nor anyone in the juvenile detention facility where he had spent six years of his life.

He did not know anything about love but he had a thorough understanding of the concept of loyalty. He knew that his total loyalty to the "Family" gave him protection from rival families. He knew that loyalty to the family gave him money and stature within the family. He was satisfied that money and respect were a fair exchange for his loyalty.

Money was useful in that it allowed him to buy some luxury items and an okay place to live in. The real payoff, in his mind, was the respect that his loyalty had earned for him in the family. Respect; now that was something he understood and treasured. It filled a fierce need within his psyche that he was not even aware existed. Nurturing and guarding the respect he had earned was a central core of Tony's existence.

To the Martorano Mafia Family Tony Scarfano was just another "soldier" albeit one whose loyalty to the family had been proven many times over. Tony had moved up through the soldier ranks starting with driving then to robberies to strong-arm stuff and now to hit man. He had earned his respect.

Then came this love that he was not even aware of.

Marie DelGato was the niece of Little Augie Martorano the Capo de Capo of the Martorano Family. As part of the inner-family circle Marie appeared at all the family rituals; weddings, baptisms, funerals, and birthdays she was always there. For years Tony Scarfano had barely noticed her. In a vague sort of way he had always thought of her as "being above him" in the family hierarchy—not that he had much interest in girls anyway.

His attitude towards Marie started to change when he had been ordered to drive Marie, her mother and two sisters home from a wedding. The mother and sisters sat in the back seat of the car and Marie in the front passenger seat. During the drive, the three women in the back seat chatted amongst themselves so Marie started a conversation with Tony. They only made small talk, but she smiled at him several times, and in a way, that made him feel warm all over. Her image and smile stayed with Tony long after the drive was over.

He began to seek her out at other family events. She always seemed glad to see him and favored him with that smile of hers. Eventually Tony began to notice that Marie would often stay close to, or dance with, Philly Sutera as if she was trying to get his attention. Philly Sutera had a lot going for him. He was handsome, in an Italian Movie star kind of way, and Tony knew he had loads of money. For a while, Tony was confused about Marie's intentions;

she was friendly and often smiled at him, but she was doing the same with Philly.

In time, Tony got up the nerve to ask Marie if she would go to dinner and a movie with him. She smiled and said, "Of course. I'd love to."

Their friendship grew from that beginning to a more consistent relationship. But always in the background, there was Philly Sutera. He was at all the family events and Marie persisted in trying to get his attention. Tony was aware of her attraction to Philly but he told himself he was gaining the upper hand with her. Didn't they go to ball games and the fights together? Didn't Marie make it a point to dance with him at every opportunity, even when Philly was around?

In time, Tony began to make plans for the day when he and Marie could be together on a permanent basis. He would leave the family and get a regular job. *Someday there would be a wedding* he thought. Anything seemed possible...until the day he heard of Marie's engagement to Philly Sutera.

I've been played! he thought. *She used me to make Philly notice her! Everyone in the family must have seen it and realized she was making a fool of me. That cagna. Betrayal was the ultimate disrespect.* It was more than he could bear.

That was why he was waiting outside her apartment.

THE HAPPY HELMET

Author's note: I wrote this story in 2016. Recent advances in Artificial Intelligence and Robotics makes the invention of a Happy Helmet or something like it, probable within the next decade. Be warned.

My life is in the dumps Jerry thought. My job is going nowhere, I don 't have any social life, I am feeling depressed, I don 't feel well, nothing has any meaning for me anymore. Life hardly seems worth living.

He slumped into the living room, plopped down on the couch, and spent another mindless evening watching mindless TV. The next two days followed the same routine.

On the fourth day, when he arrived home from work, he found a large box leaning against his front door, There was no address on the box; just the words "open me."

printed across the top. Somewhat confused, Jerry carried the box into his living room and decided not to open it until after dinner.

Jerry carefully opened the box, not knowing what to expect. Inside he found an envelope with the words "from Cyber Emotions Inc., 137 Powell St. San Francisco, CA." on it. Under the envelope, there was, what appeared to be, a football helmet. He took the helmet out of the box and examined it. As near as he could tell it was a high quality, expensive looking, professional football helmet. Its only strange characteristic was a USB port on the backside of the helmet. The box also contained a cable and charger just like the one Jerry used for his cell phone.

His curiosity now fully aroused, Jerry opened the envelope. The letter read:

Cyber Emotions Inc

987 Powell St.

San Francisco, CA 94108

Dear Recipient,

Greetings from Cyber Emotions Inc. We are a computer based start-up company that specializes in bringing together the latest technologies in computers and some advanced thinking from the fields of Psychology and Human Behavior.

For the past five years we have been developing a system for enhancing human emotions. From a combination of crowd sourcing and venture capitalists we have raised eleven million dollars and are almost ready to go into production with the system we have developed. That system is manifested in the helmet you found in this box. The last test of our system consists of getting some people to try our system for one month and then tell us about their experiences.

To make our test completely random, we have left boxes, such as the one you received, at some anonymously chosen houses in the Bay area.

Our hope is that you will agree to participate in this study. Again, all we ask is that you try this system for thirty days, and then tell us about your experiences.

By way of assurance, we can confirm to you that the helmet is completely safe to use. There is absolutely no chance of any physical harm coming to you from the helmet. You need only charge it up in any wall socket using the cable and charger we have provided. The helmet will sound a tone when its needs recharging. It is truly a plug and play system.

Your compensation for participating in the study is that you may keep the helmet at the end of the trial period. We are convinced you will find it a useful asset in your life.

Thank you for your cooperation and assistance in this important work.

Anthony Damian
Anthony Damian, CEO
Cyber Emotions Inc.

Jerry put the helmet and letter aside for a week while he considered what to do about this strange situation. Finally, Jerry decided to try it. What the heck, he thought, the way my life is going, what have I got to loose.

After dinner that evening he charged up the helmet, turned off the TV and sat down in his most comfortable chair. He very carefully put on the helmet. The inside lining was slightly warm and not at all uncomfortable. A very soft hum came to his ears; however, it was so low that he quickly forgot it was there, Gradually, he relaxed and waited to see what would come next. The warmth of the helmet and the soft hum in his ears caused him to doze off.

He slept for about twenty minutes and then woke with a start. Something had changed, but he could not say exactly what it was. He sat perfectly still for a bit trying to figure out what was different about his feelings and the mood of the room. He felt fine and free of any anxiety. His mood had definitely changed, and for the better; but his mind couldn't grasp what his new mood was or how it had come about—but he liked the new feeling. Puzzled about what had happened he took off the helmet and decided that was enough of a trial for one night. He went to bed feeling totally relaxed and had the best nights sleep he had had in months.

Jerry used the helmet for the next six evenings: each time for a longer and longer period and with growing confidence. Every time he used the helmet he felt a pleasant mood change and a growing sense of optimism. He began to believe that his life was taking on more and more meaning and usefulness.

By the end of the second week his world had changed to a very pleasant place.

His work seemed to become meaningful, and he started to develop friendships as a result of his new found charm and enthusiasm for life.

By the end of the third week, Jerry was wearing the helmet to bed at night and while working. He explained this peculiarity to his co-workers by saying that he was participating in a research study for a medical program. Once, during that week, he was sure he saw another person on the street wearing the same kind of helmet as his. He smiled to think that someone else was enjoying the same benefits he was getting from his.

At the end of the thirty-day trial period, Jerry decided not to report to the Cyber Emotions Company...he was afraid they might renege on their promise that he could keep the helmet. It had become an important, no crucial, part of his life. He could not bear the thought of living without it and the possibility of returning to his former life of apathy and anwie.

Six months later, it was common to see other people on the street wearing similar helmets.

One year later Jerry estimated that ninety percent of the population in the San Francisco Bay Area were wearing Happy Helmets.

Alternative story endings. You, dear reader, may choose whichever ending to this story you wish.

STORY ENDING NUMBER ONE

Within five years the entire human population of planet earth was wearing the Happy Helmet. This became possible when every country instituted a system of subsidies that allowed everyone to purchase a helmet. This happened when Governments realized that by making their citizens happy the government would remain in power forever since there were no complaints against it.

The earth became a place of perpetual happiness due to the Helmet's ability to change anger into complacency, frustration into accommodation, challenge into acceptance and so on. Anger, frustration challenge and all other human motions lost their meaning and their function in the course of human evolution.

No longer were there any wars, bigotry, xenophobia, nationalism or social hierarchies.

Once the concept of total everlasting happiness became imbedded in the human psyche the notion of a happy life after death as a reward for following one or another religious doctrine began to fade. Eventually, all religions vanished from human consciousness. In their place the inventors of the Happy Helmet became revered figures throughout the world.

Charles Darwin not withstanding human evolution came to a halt.

STORY ENDING NUMBER TWO

Within five years the entire human population of planet earth was wearing the Happy Helmet. This became possible when every country instituted a system of subsidies that allowed everyone to purchase a helmet. This happened when Governments realized that by making their citizens happy the government would remain in power forever since there were no complaints against it.

The earth became a virtual Garden of Eden in which the human mind, free from anger, frustration, war, bigotry xenophobia, nationalism and social hierarchies, was allowed to expand it's capabilities beyond imagination.

The Arts, medical science, all the fields of human relationships moved to never before seen heights due to the expansion and liberation of the human mind.

Once the concept of total everlasting happiness became imbedded in the human psyche the notion of a happy life after death as a reward for following one or another religious doctrine began to fade. Eventually, all religions vanished from human consciousness. In their place the inventors of the Happy Helmet became revered figures throughout the world as liberators of the full powers of the human mind.

Charles Darwin's Theory of Evolution had been put on steroids due to the Happy Helmet.

THE HAPPY PARADE

"Dad, where are we? This doesn't look like Wisconsin."

"I don't know for sure, Tommy."

"But what is this place?"

"I can't answer that either, son. But it looks like a nice enough place. Look at that beautiful blue sky. And the weather is fine."

"Yeah, Dad, I guess so. But I think I'd rather be home in Wisconsin"

"Look at all the other people here. Everybody is moving in the same direction. Let's follow them and see what we can find out."

Father and son followed the crowd and soon found themselves standing on the curb of what looked like a suburban street. Most of the people they had been following also took their places on the curb, as if waiting for a parade to come by. The father chatted with some of the nearby people, but nobody seemed to know where they were or what was going to happen. There was an air of excitement and expectation all about.

Presently, music, as if from a marching band, could be heard in the distance. The people in the crowd began craning their necks and looking up the street.

It was a parade! And a very happy one. The music was lively; there were clowns, jugglers. and people in gay costumes walking on stilts. The marchers were waving to the crowd, and the crowd was waving back and laughing. Everyone seemed to be having a grand old time.

The first group of marchers was dressed like old Greeks and Romans with flowing togas and sandals. Next came a group of courtly ladies and knights in shining armor carrying swords and shields. They were followed by more clowns and tumbling acrobats. Then came farm families in rough clothing and carrying old-fashioned wooden farm tools such as might be seen in a museum.

From time to time, a group of marchers would burst into joyous song accompanied by much laughter and applause from the spectators.

The father and son looked up the street. There seemed to be no end to the parade. The farmers and knights were followed by men and women wearing white collars and leg stockings. They looked like New England Pilgrims dressed for Thanksgiving.

"Dad, look, look! That man looks like George Washington. Could it really be him?

"Well, I don't know, Tommy, but you're right. He sure looks like President Washington."

Next came men dressed like pioneers in buckskin tunics and women in sunbonnets and long skirts. Mixed in with the pioneers were Indians in bright blankets and feathers. More farmers came along, then miners and factory workers and a large contingent of Civil War soldiers. Their marching band played "The Battle Hymn of the Republic" and "Nearer My God to Thee."

"Look Dad," Tommy said. "Those men are dressed like World War I soldiers."

"I see them," the father replied. "And this next group looks like the soldiers and sailors from World War II. If I didn't know better, I'd say that man looks like my old army buddy Jim O'Brien. But I know Jim is dead. He died in my arms."

"Dad, Dad, look—there's Grandpa! And Grandma is with him!"

Father and son stepped off the curb and began to march along with the older couple.

"Pop, what are you and Mom doing here?" the father asked. "Where are we? And where is this parade going?"

"Well, I don't know for sure, son, but mother and I have been waiting a long time for you and Tommy to join us. We're glad you're here now. As for where this parade is going, I don't know that either, but we're having such a good time we just keep on marching along with it. Wherever it's going, it must be a pretty nice place. Why don't you and Tommy stay with us?"

They did,

And the happy-parade keeps marching along.

www.ingramcontent.com/pod-product-compliance
Lightning Source LLC
Chambersburg PA
CBHW052015020726
47501CB00004B/1075